GRIM TALES

ESSEX

Edited by Luke Chapman

First published in Great Britain in 2015 by:

 Young**Writers**

Remus House
Coltsfoot Drive
Peterborough
PE2 9BF
Telephone: 01733 890066
Website: www.youngwriters.co.uk

Printed and bound in the UK by BookPrintingUK
Website: www.bookprintinguk.com

FOREWORD

Welcome, Reader!

For Young Writers' latest competition, Grim Tales, we gave secondary school pupils nationwide the tricky task of writing a story with a beginning, middle and an end in just 100 words. They could either write a completely original tale or add a twist to a well-loved classic. They rose to the challenge magnificently!

We chose stories for publication based on style, expression, imagination and technical skill. The result is this entertaining collection full of diverse and imaginative mini sagas, which is also a delightful keepsake to look back on in years to come.

Here at Young Writers our aim is to encourage creativity in young adults and to inspire a love of the written word, so it's great to get such an amazing response, with some absolutely fantastic stories. This made it a tough challenge to pick the winners, so well done to Abigail McNaught who has been chosen as the best author in this anthology.

I'd like to congratulate all the young authors in Grim Tales - Essex - I hope this inspires them to continue with their creative writing. And who knows, maybe we'll be seeing their names on the best seller lists in the future...

Jenni Bannister

Editorial Manager

CONTENTS

The Coopers Company & Coborn School, Upminster

The King John School, Benfleet

The Palmer Catholic Academy, Ilford

Trinity School, Brentwood

Valentines High School, Ilford

THE
MINI SAGAS

THE MAIDEN WHO DROWNED ON THE SHORE

Rosalind felt every grain of sand beneath her feet. The tips of her fair locks were damp. If she squinted she could make out shadows darting across the ocean. Rosalind resented the fact she was confined to the tower, she longed to be with the mysterious and dangerous creatures in the water. 'Hello! Are you there?' she cried. The sea rose, Rosalind stepped back yet it kept crawling up the shore. Voices hissed, trespassers as the waves consumed her. Mermaids, in a flash of scales and fangs the girl's ruined body sank. Rosalind lay dead amongst the seaweed and fish.

THEOLA OJO (12)

ALICE

Alice, Alice was a lost soul. She fell down a rabbit hole. Blame her parents, blame herself. Blame the rabbits, it was just bad health. The syringes of joy and the pills of goodwill. She had a few demons in a hole she couldn't fill. Felt like she could talk to no one, she needed to escape, escape and have fun. She talked of a hatter, a cat and a queen. Everyone thought she was a deluded teen. Alice was in Wonderland for most of her life, whoever thought it would end with a knife.

SEBASTIAN SANCHEZ
Clacton County High School, Clacton-On-Sea

Into The Darkness

We stepped up to the big, wooden door as scared as each other, our minds as chilled as the icy metal door handle. We opened the door and plunged into the darkness. Strange, it was very concerning really, just one room, one door, one mirror, one... one, 'Run!' screamed James. 'Turn and run.' We all started to hide.
After 10 minutes I stood up to find four puddles of blood, four bodies, yet there were only four of us to start with. The woman in the mirror was the headline. With nothing to use as evidence I slowly gave up.

Ollie Palmer (13)
Clacton County High School, Clacton-On-Sea

Homicide

The noise gets louder and louder until the machines fall silent. We get led like sheep into this death camp. The blood that drips is ripe, red it drips from the freshly cut necks, necks of regret. Our pink skin gets pierced with syringes of joy. Our faces light up for the last time, the blood protrudes, it drips down our hair, we get painted red. Our soul runs down the drain. Our life gone.

Kofi Wells
Clacton County High School, Clacton-On-Sea

THE PACKAGE . . .

Hello my name is Alex, I am a lonely old man who lives in an ordinary house in an ordinary country (England). One day my life changed forever, this is how it happened. I was sitting in my arm chair when the door rang, I thought it was them rotten kids again knocking on my door and running away. I ran to the door hoping to catch them, however it was something different, very different, so terrifying and scary I almost wet my pants...

ALEX BROWN (13)
Clacton County High School, Clacton-On-Sea

BAA BAA BLACK SHEEP HAS NO LONGER ANY WOOL

Baa Baa Black Sheep has no longer any wool. He was a nice, kind sheep, full of beans. He would let anyone have his fluffy wool (only the people who paid that is). Black Sheep was strolling through town, the wind weaving through his wool... Baa Baa's now a chilly sheep, his skin as bear as night. He was shaved and punched and thrown in the streets for warmth he relies on a jumper!

HARRY McCARTHY (13)
Clacton County High School, Clacton-On-Sea

PORRIDGE

You have all heard the tale of Goldilocks and the three bears, here's the correct version ... When the bears came home and found Goldilocks you could hear somebody sleeping in the bed. She tried to run, her fear and heart pounding as fast as a racing car. She got up and charged for the door but Daddy Bear was too quick for Goldilocks. He grabbed her and said, 'I see you've ate all the porridge, so I can only do one thing...' That night they had a bowl of porridge with goldisyrup.

MILLIE ROSE FREE (12)
Clacton County High School, Clacton-On-Sea

THE MOON MUST FALL

Blade across the skin, blood on the floor, blood on my dress, her blood on my hands. Ella the beautiful Ella, the Ella that basks in glory and fame, the Ella that made me ugly, the Ella that now lay cold on the floor. We were beautiful little stars but then the moon appeared, she planned to kill the king, to take the golden throne and run the town into ruin. I was only trying to save him from the nightmare about to be told. Though the moon is beautiful, it is gone for the sun is to rise.

AMBER COPPIN
Clacton County High School, Clacton-On-Sea

RAPUNZEL

One day in Bush Town, there was a girl called Rapunzel. Her great, great, great, great grand horse told her she was allowed to go out to the park with her African friends, so they could make some cakes. Later on when her friends came, they brought their friends, the three little scrubs, so they could help out. Meanwhile, she was getting dressed up in her tracksuit with many holes in. As soon as she came down with her hair, unfortunately she slipped and she fell down the tower and landed on her head.

VICTOR EIGBE (12)
Colchester Academy, Colchester

FOX AND THE HOUND

I was born, and two days later came one man with a rifle and one ferocious dog. They were fox hunters, after me and my mum. She ran away with me in her mouth. She hid me behind a fence post and she ran and left me behind. I waited a whole day but my mother never came back. Now I'm okay, I have my best friend Copper the hound, my wife and best of all my two pups Olly and Lucky.

ARCHIE CLEWLEY (12)
Colchester Academy, Colchester

RUMPELSTILTSKIN

The old man offered his daughter to the king in the promise she could produce large amounts of gold. The king ordered her to produce gold or she would be executed. She sat and cried. A short man in green called Rumpelstiltskin appeared and said, 'Don't cry I will make gold if you give me everything you own.'
'That would be really conspicuous so no,' she said. Rumple vanished and she was executed.

OLLIE JAMES TANDY (12)
Colchester Academy, Colchester

DEAD WHITE

A girl lived in a palace with her stepmother. Her stepmother was evil and tried to kill Snow White many a time. One day though she thought of something horrible. Poison Snow in her sleep. That night she was waiting in her room and as soon as she was asleep, *bang!* A lamp crashed to the floor. Luckily, Snow didn't awake from her slumber. The poison went into her mouth. When Snow didn't awake that morning her stepmother pretended to be upset, but she knew deep down that she had done wrong and her dead daughter would get her revenge.

CASEY WALSH (11)
Colchester Academy, Colchester

WRECKY RAPUNZEL

Rapunzel lived in an old tower at the top of Barry Lane. She loved her life there. She had a wicked mother, had a frog father and a wooden brother. Rapunzel had cut her red hair short and she loved it, she was always going out to hang out with her friends at the police station. She often did this. While Rapunzel was sharpening her knives one day she heard a horse neigh so she checked what it was and the horse was there right in front of her. She was so scared she fainted, never to be awake again.

KAUSARA AYOOLA (12)
Colchester Academy, Colchester

THE MUD PIE

The pigs screamed, I ran inside the house. They would soon knock it down with their massive bellies. My three young wolf pups would be thrown in mud. I would rather be eaten. I hate the mud so much. I love having the pigs as neighbours and as friends but no mud. The pigs asked me if they could come in, but not by the fur of the cubs. They broke the door and my poor house down and took me and my pups into the mud. What I didn't know is my wolf cubs and I were their lunch.

SHANNON MEAKINS
Colchester Academy, Colchester

BEAUTY AND THE WHAT?

She knocked on the door. Silent was the forest. Among her stood a 20ft tall castle, her father had gone and she found his horse on the path, leading to the castle. She decided to open the door with her own strength. Then she saw a beautifully presented set of stairs, she decided to go up them. She was calling for her father, however, there was no reply. Then behind her she saw a shadow – what was it?

ELLA-MARIE LIUZZI COGAN (12)
Colchester Academy, Colchester

CINDERELLA

Cinderella worked in her stepmother's castle doing the chores and working as a slave. One day, an invitation came to the castle to invite the women in the town to a ball. Cinderella's stepmother locked Cinderella in her room. The coach came to pick them up, Jaq and Gus unlocked the door but Cinderella's dress was ruined. Cinderella's fairy godmother turned up but turned Jaq and Gus into beautiful women. The newly formed women raced to the prince, had a lovely time, but midnight came and the women tuned back into Jaq and Gus.

REBECCA LEE (11)
Colchester Academy, Colchester

Kensuke's Kingdom

My football fell out of my hands. Stella, my dog, jumped into the deep, blue ocean to get it. I put on my life jacket and jumped to rescue my stranded dog out of the ocean. The yacht left us behind. We were both alone and cold, floating on my football. 'Help!' I screamed. But we received no help. I knew now that the only way to survive was to float until we hit land and try to survive from that point onwards until my parents came to rescue me with the yacht that we liked to call, 'Peggy Sue'.

Lukas Daulenskis (12)
Colchester Academy, Colchester

Rapunzel

'I'm here!' came an anonymous voice from below, a flock of blonde hair fell down from the narrowed window, the anonymous person climbed up the tower and descended into the eerie tower. He, the anonymous, crept carefully towards the tower even more but then he heard a noise of agony from behind. He turned around, it was an old lady, but he knew the sound was not from her, she was hiding something, she was holding a knife behind her back, he knew it had to somehow escape, but what was that hideous noise he heard earlier?

Robin Rai (12)
Colchester Academy, Colchester

THE THREE KIDS' TALE

There was a field, a big dip in the ground and the only way to get across it was to go down and up. I went first, I got there, had a look over and saw a big giant down there sleeping. We had to help each other to get across. We built a big ladder which was big, another to get across but we had to be very quiet or he would wake up. We put the ladder across... *Crash!* We all looked at the giant, he was still asleep, we got across and played all day long.

JAKE CROSSLEY (11)
Colchester Academy, Colchester

RAPUNZEL REMIX

A prince in the forest hears a voice like no other, he follows the sound to a tower. A beautiful maiden with long hair sits at the window. The tower has no windows or doors. He shouts to the maiden, 'What is your name?'
She replies, 'Rapunzel is my name!' She then follows with, 'Would you like to come in?'
'I can't my love there is no door!' She looks down and clicks her fingers, the wall departs to create a doorway. He walks in, the wall closes then the room gets smaller, there's no way out...

ELLIANNA STEWART
Colchester Academy, Colchester

RAPUNZEL

'Rapunzel, Rapunzel let down your hair,' shouted Rapunzel's mum. 'No, I hate you, I really, really hate you, get lost,' came the startled voice from the tower. Rapunzel's mother went to town to fetch a ladder and out popped a prince in torn clothes. The prince asked Rapunzel to let down her hair. This time she agreed. The prince started climbing but what Rapunzel didn't know was who the prince was...

ALICIA MURPHY (12)
Colchester Academy, Colchester

ALICE IN WONDERLAND FAIL

The white rabbit ran past poor Alice, confused she followed him to an old tree stump. She looked surprised as the rabbit said, 'I'm very late for an important date!'
She thought no more, down the stump poor Alice fell. She followed, she fell she hit her head then came Wonderland. She stumbled and saw people with flamingoes as croquet bats, giant jam tarts then the Queen of Hearts shouting, 'Where are my tarts as I'm the Queen of Hearts.' Poor Alice awoke confused, she got up and ran.

ELOISE THURLOW (12)
Colchester Academy, Colchester

LITTLE RED RIDING HOOD

In the forest I saw her skipping along the green grass with a red hood. A brown basket and nice cakes and bread. Still watching her I saw an old style house, I saw Grandma in her old, warm bed. I then ate her up and put the old robe on and got in her bed. Then there was a knock at the door. Red Riding Hood was here and started being mean to me, I started to run out of the door and ran so I didn't come back.

HARRY LOVELL-MURPHY (14)
Colchester Academy, Colchester

RAPUNZEL

There once was an evil stepmother that was locked in a high castle with an annoying ferret. Rapunzel lived a perfect life with her two best friends, Mr Rabbit and the Clumsy Dragon. The step mother had to do everything Rapunzel said. This was Rapunzel's revenge after all those years that evil step mother kept her in that castle, she had no life or no contact with anyone. Then that day came when Rapunzel got set free and the evil step mother put a curse on the castle forever, she locked herself in the castle forever for lying.

KAY NEWMAN (13)
Colchester Academy, Colchester

ALADDIN

There was a street rat, he was called Aladdin, he was a diamond in the rough. He went to the café to collect the award he was promised. He did not know lurking in the corner was the old king, Aladdin. He got out of the café and passed the king and ran away. He had Genie in his grasp. Aladdin made the genie do bad because he wanted to become the new lord and destroy the world.

TRINITY SLATER (14)
Colchester Academy, Colchester

BEAUTY AND THE BEAST

There is this girl called Belle. She went in to town and returned her book that she got from the library. Then she went back home to see her father, but he was working on something, but it blew up. Belle's father went somewhere to show his work to people, then he got in a fight with the wolves and he lost his horse. Then he came across a castle. The horse took Belle to where her father was. Belle loves her dad and would do anything for him.

BRYANNA SMITH (13)
Colchester Academy, Colchester

THE GINGERBREAD MAN

An old man and an old woman made gingerbread men. One of the gingers came alive, the gingerbread man ran down the road. The old man and the old woman chased him. Little did he know a fox was waiting by the river. The little gingerbread man stopped, he knew he couldn't get across so he asked the fox if he could go across the river on his back. The fox agreed then the gingerbread man ran on longer after that, the fox sprinted and ate him up in one mouthful. They were very sad.

CORI-ANNE NICHOLSON (14)
Colchester Academy, Colchester

HOOK'S BIG BITE

I am a boy like no other, I am a boy so special I can fly. One day whilst flying I was caught by a net and hit the ground. I woke up in a room with the face of the preposterous hook. He is dancing with glee, is this the end? No, I am the great, I challenge him to a duel – I try to feed him to the crocs but the water suddenly freezes.

KAI BOKENHAM (14)
Colchester Academy, Colchester

The Story Of Shrekpunzel

Once upon a time there was a young girl called Rapunzel. She had really long, blonde hair that was as bright as the sun. She was abandoned by her mum and was looked after by an old lady. She told her she was her mother and she didn't let Rapunzel out of the tower. One day Rapunzel escaped from the tower and found a dragon. After she got on the dragon, Shrek came along and destroyed the tower. She fell and died by falling into a ditch.

RYAN BRILEY (13)
Colchester Academy, Colchester

Rapunzel!

Once upon a fairytale there was a young, bright, blonde, gorgeous girl who lived in a tower. One day a man came and rescued her from the wicked witch who used Rapunzel's hair to stay and look young. The witch had locked Rapunzel in the tower to keep her hidden. The prince was a life saver as he saved her from the wicked witch. He was so handsome and he was dressed in scruffy clothes but that didn't matter to Rapunzel. Rapunzel married the prince and thankfully she lived happily ever after with the scruffy, gorgeous, handsome, annoying, pretty prince.

HOLLY MORRISSON (13)
Colchester Academy, Colchester

HUNTED

Crack! The wolf was curious of the noise. He went to go see if it was his dinner. It wasn't. A girl in a silky, red hood turned and looked at the wolf. The girl said, 'Boo!' The wolf scattered with fear. He didn't look back at the girl. She walked back to her nan's. The wolf never returned, the forest never felt the same again. On a cold day the wolf started to walk clueless back to the forest. Was the girl there? No. Any red around? No. He was safe for now. There was a bang! No wolf.

JORDAN MANNING (13)
Colchester Academy, Colchester

RED RIDING HOOD

Once upon a time there was a little girl called Red Riding Hood, she was hanging the washing up when her mum came out and said, 'Here are some cookies for Grandma, run along now, don't be late home please there are weirdos about.' She set off through the woods when she heard a howl and she stopped dead. She felt warmth come towards her. She turned around and there was a wolf stood with slobber dripping from his teeth, Mrs Little Red Riding Hood fell with shock and the wolf scoffed all the cookies but he was still hungry.

CAITLIN WOODCOCK (12)
Colchester Academy, Colchester

WOLF

There was a little girl who wore a red hood which was a jacket and it was red too. She was on the way to her nan's house, the house was made with bricks, with stars on the top and it was brown on top. She picked some things for her nan because her nan was not as well as she should be. She would let someone in her house, if she thought she knew them, but she didn't. She was so ill she got eaten by the wolf.

KELSIE HEFFRON (12)
Colchester Academy, Colchester

LITTLE RED RIDING HOOD AND THE WOLF

The wolf could hear twigs snapping through the woods. It smelt of human. He ran after the human. When he laid eyes on the human he could see the shiny axe covered with shoe polish. He was big and bald. The human was a lumberjack, he watched as he chopped down trees. Later a girl with a hood came into his sight. She went to a log cabin. An old lady lived there. But out of nowhere an axe hit the wolf.

JORDON MOSS (13)
Colchester Academy, Colchester

I'm Not Loony Or Lying!

The old blacksmith spent the week making a puppet. One night he finished it but he was so tired he slept. Another day came, the puppet was missing. He searched the whole workshop, but it wasn't there. The old blacksmith looked towards the window, the puppet was sitting still as a feather looking at two children playing. He came alive and wanted to play but no one let him. People thought the puppet was crazy for 'pretending to be a puppet'. After 2 years of loneliness the puppet turned to a statue outside the window of the workshop.

DAVID GAO (13)
Colchester Academy, Colchester

Red Riding Hood

Belle, cleaning every speck of dust, singing along happily. She realises her dad has not returned, she goes out looking for him. She finds his cart and the horses trying to break free, she looks up to see a figure standing holding her dad in the air. She begs for him to be released she'll stay instead, it's a beast. The only way she could be released is if she kissed him, staying there for a long time, finally she was free! She returned home knowing she made the beast a man again, she was free forever.

LIANA GREEN (12)
Colchester Academy, Colchester

THE ANIMAL

Crash! There was a noise in the forest. Wolf smell was in the air, but I carried on walking. Then an animal jumped out of the bush. Then an axe man came along and killed him. I carried on my way to grandma's house. But then another crash came from her house. I busted the door down and there was a wolf, but I just killed it and gave grandma her lunch. Then another wolf came and ate us, but at that same moment the axe man came in and freed us. So we had dinner with the man.

LUKE BRUNDELL (13)
Colchester Academy, Colchester

SNOW WHITE

Once upon a time there was a little girl, her hair was as black as the night, her skin was white as snow. Her mum passed away during labour, her name was Snow White. Her dad grew up with Snow White helping him. The king decided to get a new lover. He thought it would help the family. He went on a mission. Snow White had grown so much, Snow White was staying with her stepmum, who she didn't know was evil. Snow White was happy as ever but the stepmum was trying to kill Snow White.

CHLOE LOUISE MCGOWAN (13)
Colchester Academy, Colchester

CINDERELLA WITH A TWIST

It was party night. Cinderella wasn't allowed to go. She was mad. She crept into her stepmum's room with a knife. Blood everywhere. Cinderella chucked her out the window The stepsisters left quickly because they saw everything.

The next day the police bundled through the door and arrested Cinderella. She was trialled a week later and sentenced to life in a prison cell. After thirty years she was moved to Villain Town prison. At the age of forty she escaped. She jumped through the metal bars, she was never seen or found again after that eventful night in November 1981.

MILLIE GRANT (12)
Colchester Academy, Colchester

BELLE AND THE BEAST

There was a young girl called Belle. Belle walked to the huge tower and knocked on the door, *creak,* the door opened. Belle walked in with fright, she arrived at the top of the castle and found a bright, red rose. 'Get out of my castle!' a beast shouted.

'Argh!' Belle ran downstairs.

Two hours later Belle realised that all the beast needed was a true love's kiss. Belle and the beast had a long conversation and started falling in love with each other.

One year later the beast was married to Belle. And they lived happily ever after.

PORTIA SPINDLER (12)
Colchester Academy, Colchester

LITTLE RED RIDING HOOD

There once was a girl called Little Red Riding Hood, who dressed up in all red. One day she went to her grandmother's house because her grandmother was ill. On her way there, the path was blocked so she had to walk through the woods. When she walked through the woods, she heard a snapping sound on the bark, so she quickly ran to her grandmother's house. When she got there, she walked through the door, but suddenly saw a wolf so she let out a big scream and the wolf ran out of the small Victorian cottage.

DYLAN JACOBS (13)
Colchester Academy, Colchester

LITTLE RED RIDING HOOD

Crash! There was a sound in the forest. The wolf heard a noise. He went to go and find out who is in the forest. He found the intruder. The big bad wolf hid behind a tree and saw a little, delicious looking girl in a red hood. He howled and the little girl heard it. She ran as fast as she could to her gran's house, but when she got there her gran wasn't there. When she tried to find out where she went the wolf was right behind her and she knew it. He ate her very quickly.

ZAK COLIN JOHNSON-HARDCASTLE (13)
Colchester Academy, Colchester

HUNGRY HUNTER

A flash whizzed past his face. He glared at the red light, a cloak flowing backwards into the air showing a basket of cookies. He glared at them and suddenly he jumped and grabbed one and stealthily landed on the other side of the path. He took a humongous bite into the cookie and he loved it! He howled as loud as every wolf alive. He took a close look at the girl and the he saw a beam of light from a badge. He took a closer look and it said, 'Little Red Riding Hood.'

DEIVIS SAVELJEVAS (13)
Colchester Academy, Colchester

NOT SO WONDERLAND!

As I run through the hedgerow my blue, laced dress sways around, ripping and tearing from the thorns in the hedge. As I follow the flash of white, I try and keep out of sight. Suddenly, I find myself falling into a crazy world I see in my dreams. But something is different, the hatter's not mad, there is only one twin and he is tall and thin. The rabbit's got a fork and is trying to stab me, the Cheshire cat is not appearing. The Queen of Hearts is really good. Oh my gosh I must be mad!

HOLLY BURMAN (12)
Colchester Academy, Colchester

THE FALL AT THE BALL

Ding-dong! The clock struck 12. I had to run. I knew the glass slippers wouldn't hold my weight, they smashed, stabbing me in the foot. I was in shock as I fell back and heard a crack as my back hit the marble steps. Blood dripping from my head and my foot, unable to move I just lay there, helpless. I lay in a pool of blood, my gown ruined, my hair dripping wet. I hoped the prince would come and he did and that's why I'm still here, today, alive and living happily ever after.

MADISON BOUGHTON (11)
Colchester Academy, Colchester

TRICKSTER

Shrek lives in a swamp. One day Lord Farquaad comes and fills Shrek's swamp with fairytale characters. He meets Donkey and does a deal with Farquaad to get a princess. He climbs mountains and rivers. All Donkey does is talk, so Shrek says, 'Shut up!' He leaves his job and pretends to have the princess. Shrek tricks Farquaad and kills him. The princess is rescued by someone else. Donkey goes and lives on a farm and Shrek goes and lives in his lovely and beautiful swamp forever.

CAUNOR GREGO (13)
Colchester Academy, Colchester

LITTLE RED HOOD

Little Red Hood is taking a basket of cookies to her Grandma. She gets to the door and goes in, she then bumps into her grandma but at that moment Grandma turns into a wolf. The wolf chases her all around the forest. Red Hood finds a woodsman. She goes to him for protection but he can't hear or see her. Eventually he turns around but his axe hits Red Hood and she dies. The wolf then catches up and kills the woodsman. Finally the wolf turns back into the grandma and realises what she has done.

RHIAN THOMPSON (13)
Colchester Academy, Colchester

THE GINGERBREAD MAN

'Charge!' Before he knew it an army of gingerbread men came charging at him. The fox ran as fast as he could but however fast he ran he couldn't escape. He felt a pair of tiny arms on his legs slowing him down. He was surrounded by gingerbread men seeking vengeance. Suddenly, the circle around him made a space, a half eaten gingerbread man walked up to him, 'You're finished!' He took out a knife sharper than two razors. He injected the knife into the fox. Blood dripped everywhere, a swarm of 50 gingerbread men took the fox's body away.

SADE BROWN
Colchester Academy, Colchester

CINDERELLA

One girl called Cinderella lived with her father. Her father married a lady and she had three kids. Later her father died and the stepmother did not like her. One day the others went to the dance and she stayed at home because she did not have good clothes. Later, one fairy appeared and made her beautiful for the dance. But she needed to come back at midnight. When she came back she lost her shoe and the prince was trying to find whose shoe it was, he found her and they lived happily forever.

PANDORA FERNANDES (12)
Colchester Academy, Colchester

HANSEL AND GINGER

The witch sensed something. The house was invaded. She got on her broom and flew to the gingerbread house. Some of the door was missing! She went inside and found two children, a boy and a girl. She slammed the door and locked it, then put the boy in a cauldron over a fire and the girl in a cage. They both tried to escape but the witch turned them into gingerbread men and ate them, but before she knew it, one of them took a swig of vinegar and then the witch exploded into a green, slimy, disgusting goop.

JAMIE WOOD (12)
Colchester Academy, Colchester

THE DISNEY CASTLE

Two little girls walked up to the grand Disney Castle. Another girl was standing outside staring at it. She sharply turned around and said, 'You're going to die in there. You will regret it.' The two smaller girls walked slowly into the castle, they arrived at the room with the princess in and burst through the door. The princess slowly turned around. They had no skin on their faces. The muscle was raw, the two girls screamed. The lights went off. There was a flash. Something went over. The light came back on...

MADDIE POULTON (11)
Davenant Foundation School, Loughton

THREE LITTLE PIGS

The pigs sat there trembling. They had lit a fire in the chimney. There was no way he was getting in. They could hear growling. They then heard him breathe in and nothing happened, he couldn't blow the house down. *Bang!* He smashed into the wall. *Bang!* He tried again, the house shook. They were surprised they were still alive. His footsteps became distant. He had run away. They heard him getting closer and *bang!* He smashed through the wall. He grabbed the pigs and threw them on a fire, he said, 'Bacon tastes better with blood.'

SIDNEY TAYLOR (11)
Davenant Foundation School, Loughton

SKYFALL

Time stopped. Blood trickled down its beak. The blood of sky gods. He sounded the alarm, he screamed. He cried, 'The sky's falling,' no one came. It intensified. Blood puddles started wailing in warning for this day would be the past, present and future, yet no one came. They stayed in the hollow oak tree, working. Hopeless in hell. They didn't move to the safe spot. The sky was falling. Blood raged on pounding the floor like skinless hands beating its victim. He dragged them out, the safe zone in sight, the rock hit the safe zone – KFC for everyone!

MATTHEW UNWIN (12)
Davenant Foundation School, Loughton

THE THREE LITTLE KIDS

There was a flash of blood coming from the woods. The three little kids were alone. Walking home alone. Then a sudden movement. A man with blood dripping down his face. It wasn't his! In the field were two little eyes staring and staring. It was just the kids, the man and the eyes – who would survive? The strange, mysterious man walked towards the kids pondering if they would survive? Or would it be dinner time for the old man. The man was never seen again and neither were the three little kids...

BETHANY REBECCA TAYLOR (12)
Davenant Foundation School, Loughton

Witch Bites The Dust

The witch turns. There is a noise. She turns. *Bang!* The noise moves again. Out of the corner of her eye, a black figure. She turns again. The figure has no head or legs, she starts slowly moving out of the room, eyes on the black figure at all times. It is moving... She's out of the room, into her cauldron she falls! 'Argh!' She stops. 'Where am I?' 'In Hell,' the voice moves, 'In Hell, in Hell, in Hell,' the voice repeats again and again.
'Stop! Who are you?'
'I am your worst nightmare.'

HANNAH WINCH (11)
Davenant Foundation School, Loughton

Destroy!

The zombies were coming. People who were once human, are now just bits of rotting flesh. They knew only one thing. Destroy! Tom was running, running faster than he had ever ran before. No matter how fast he ran or how slow they walked, they were always behind him. He was running through the remains of a ruined city. Destroyed skyscrapers were a reminder of his world. Then a zombie appeared in front of him. It lunged at him, his mouth was full of saliva, drool running down his chin. Then there were more. All he could think was destroy!

FINLAY JORDAN (12)
Davenant Foundation School, Loughton

Peter Bites Again

It was just an ordinary day for Peter Rabbit. He was off to get his lunch – human's flesh. His victim this time was Mr Dole, the one who throws stones at the rabbits at night. Peter slid under the gate. In the distance he could see Mr Dole gardening. He got closer and closer. 'Ah, ah, ah, ah,' shrieked Mr Dole. Blood, guts, skin, all down to one little rabbit. As Peter was yet to learn, Mrs Dole had seen everything, with one last hop Mrs Dole struck and Peter fell to his death bed.

Paige Charlotte Thorpe (12)
Davenant Foundation School, Loughton

Prince Charming Or Was It?

Ella was a slave. She had two evil sisters (who were secretly nice but didn't like to show it). One day Ella went riding into the deep woods. The prince saw her there and told her to come to his ball at the palace. A day later there she was standing at the ball in the most amazing gown. They stepped outside onto the glittering balcony and suddenly, the prince struck Ella with a knife in the heart. So there she was at the ball but this time she was on the ground in a gown of blood.

Grace Marsh (11)
Davenant Foundation School, Loughton

THE DISNEY NIGHTMARE

All the Disney characters were gathering together as usual. They were busy solving each other's problems! 'Argh!' A deafening scream. They turned in unison, discovering a mysterious girl! Straggly hair, talons, red eyes! 'Flee as soon as you can!' she wailed sharply. Confused! Worried! Stricken! 'It's coming – I'm coming.' 'Poor girl must be delirious,' exclaimed Wolf. Nevertheless they picked themselves up – in unison and slowly retreated.
'Phew they're gone!' sneered the mysterious six-year-old. Now her and Snow White (six years old) could play together.
'Let's play wolf!'
'Don't worry – I'll be wolf,' mocked the mysterious girl. *Pounce.* 'Argh!'

JESSIE BUSSELL (11)
Davenant Foundation School, Loughton

THE 12:00 KILLER

Jade was exhausted of working every day. She worked till she felt sweat on her forehead like a snail had crawled across her and blood covered the tips of her fingers as she scrubbed the floor. Jade wanted revenge on her mistress Daisy. The next day Jade didn't work hard as she normally did, Daisy whipped her but Jade didn't care. That night Daisy pattered upstairs to her room, she opened the door and saw Jade's eyes gleaming at her. Jade produced a knife and stabbed Daisy in the heart. 12:00, Daisy died. All was left was her bloodstained finger.

KIARA ADRIAN (12)
Davenant Foundation School, Loughton

The Unearthly Beasts

In the jungle, the group of children thought they were alone, that nobody would find them. They were wrong. They came quietly and un-noticed, being careful they didn't snap a twig until they were close. They saw their prey and moved in. It was when they surrounded the boys that they suddenly pounced, with their huge teeth and claws ready to dig into somebody's flesh. The boys' reflexes came in use when they heard the massive, brutal, destroying ogres for the first time. They ran rapidly, using every muscle and bone in their body. They could only hope to survive.

JACK SOWERBY (11)
Davenant Foundation School, Loughton

Prince Not So Charming

One mysterious day Rapunzel was sharpening her knives when she heard a male voice cry out, 'Rapunzel, Rapunzel, let down your hair.' She thought to herself, *fresh meat!* She let down her hair, and the prince climbed up. When he got into the tower Rapunzel wrapped her hair around his neck and strangled him. That was the last time Prince Charming was seen.

JESSICA ROSE SHEEHY (13)
Davenant Foundation School, Loughton

THE ASSASSIN

She leapt through the trees like a monkey. Her black body armour reflected the blinding light of the sun. Suddenly she came to a stop. Just a few metres away were two out of the eleven targets she had to hunt. She descended from the tree and whipped out her pistol. Two cocks and both of her opponents were on the floor lying in their own blood. Just behind them were four shimmers in the air. She knew those shimmers too well. In a flash she whipped out a glowing katana and sliced at thin air. Blood oozed. She vanished...

CADE CARTER THOMAS (12)
Davenant Foundation School, Loughton

THE TIGER IN THE WOODS

The pain crept across her back like needles. Her body hunched over as she turned into a beast. Every night she turned from a girl to a tiger. She crept into the woods away from all human eyes. Her stomach rumbled as she smelt the most wonderful smell. There was an 18-year-old boy all on his own. Before waiting, the tiger, forgetting her human traits, lunged at the boy. Her teeth sank into him and blood covered her yellow teeth, meanwhile dripping down her lips. Licking her lips, she walked away.

RACHEL BERRY
Davenant Foundation School, Loughton

THE THREE LITTLE MURDERERS

The police turned up. Wolf, Dog and Chains were ready. The police knocked. No answer. The door was kicked in. The first cop was stabbed in the throat and the second and third were shot with AK-47s. The police fired back with MI911's and pump action shotguns. Time to go! Wolf and Dog killed the rest whilst Chains got the van. Cops were shot in the head and a river of blood flowed into the house. They drove away. From cop cars to vans both sides were hanging out the windows, Wolf got an RPG, never seen again...

ETHAN HOLLAND (12)
Davenant Foundation School, Loughton

TAKEN

The girl was asleep until she heard a snap outside. The stairs creaked as she gently tiptoed down them. A full moon shone through the dark sky, casting an eerie glow across the garden. Another snap. Something was in the undergrowth, behind the bush. She pulled back the leaves and saw a cat. It was just a cat. Another snap. 'Mum, Dad?' she whispered. No answer. As she peered behind a second bush, skeletal fingers touched her. She crumpled to the floor. Her scream was muffled by the dark grass. Her clothes were soaked in blood. The killer took her.

MICHAEL LYONS (12)
Davenant Foundation School, Loughton

CINDERELLA

It was 5.30 when everyone found out. The prince was holding a ball to conclude final decisions for his marriage. Natasha and Terica were putting on make-up hoping to make an impression at the ball. Cinderella was getting ready in her room. Everyone was hoping to marry the prince at the ball, even Cinderella. Natasha saw Cinderella clutch the prince's hand and waltz onto the floor. She decided to get rid of her. Natasha grabbed Cinderella, locked her in a larder and grabbed the prince. The drunk prince decided to marry Natasha instead! Cinderella peered through the window and wept.

LYDIA CALLOMON (12)
Davenant Foundation School, Loughton

THE BLACK FLAMES

I sense death. It's strong... The black flames engulfed my bare bones. My scythe gleamed on my back as the flames stretched upward. My hollow eyes caught the last glimpse of the sunlight before I was enveloped inside. My eyes followed the shadow of the beast, and saw death. A girl screamed, and the scythe swung. Blood splattered the walls as the wolf split in two. The body of the gran split out of the wolf and that is when the girl lunged. She ripped me apart until I was just a pile of bones and the black flames extinguished.

AIDAN MULHOLLAND
Davenant Foundation School, Loughton

Death Of The Bumblebees!

One day, in a small village, a hive of bees suddenly changed. These bees were used to buzzing and being mischievous, however something in the air turned their little lives around. The humans that lived in the house next to the hive were loving people and loved having the bees buzzing all day. But what affected the bees affected the humans too, in just five minutes the whole house had gone mad! Finally they came outside, saw the bee hive, then... *crash! Smash! Boom!* All the bees were dead and the hive, shattered to pieces! They never saw light again.

Isabelle Levy (12)
Davenant Foundation School, Loughton

Hansel And Gretel – Witch Hunters

20 years later... Hansel and Gretel creeping in the bush with eyes on the cabin. All of a sudden they heard a voice, 'Hee, hee, hee, what do we have here, mortals?' Hansel and Gretel leapt out the bush and ran in the cabin. Hansel was aware that was a witch. Slowly walking round corners Hansel gripped tighter to his spear gun. He soon saw the witch throwing ingredients in her cauldron. Hansel took aim and shot. The spear went straight through her head and she fell in the cauldron. Soon after, the cauldron exploded, nobody was seen again.

Ioan Kamberov (11)
Davenant Foundation School, Loughton

Peter Pan's Evil Plan

There lives a man, an evil sick man. Peter Pan. He has powers, he can fly into people's dreams. Wendy's. He portrays himself as a heroic boy. He enters Wendy's dream and she fall in love with his false self. Wendy wakes with Peter by the window, step by step Wendy comes closer to her false love, Wendy leaves to Neverland. The closer the cursed pair fly, slowly Peter's true identity unravels. A monster is formed, but it's too late. Wendy is stuck in Neverland. Wendy's never getting out, she's left to die. Peter's cursed next victim awaits.

Daisy Perryer
Davenant Foundation School, Loughton

Not So Sweet Rapunzel

Innocently, the sweet girl Rapunzel glares out of her tower, waiting for her next prey to arrive. Although the local villagers never return when they try to rescue her from her evil, vile mother, little do they know it's all an act. Rapunzel has her mum and the whole village under a spell. Each and every prince, man and tramp that tries to rescue her, enter her trap. They get gruesomely strangled with her long, fine locks. All her mum can do is sit and watch hopelessly as the town frames her as the witch. Everyone around Rapunzel is doomed...

Elysia Perryer (14)
Davenant Foundation School, Loughton

HIS LOST BOYS

Bang! The window shot open, cold air streamed in to the room. A boy reaches out to the paralysed children; a twisted, devilish grin stretched across his face, he knew their pain but he didn't want to take it away. That's not what he told them though. They took his hand and his intentions became clear, but it was too late, far too late. The moment he stepped in to the room, they were already gone, they're now his lost boys. Forever forgotten. Forever lifeless, forever waiting for someone.

NICOLE HOOKE (13)
Davenant Foundation School, Loughton

BANG GOES THE SNOW

As the fair Snow White walked up to the unknown house, she took a deep breath and walked in. As the door cracked open she heard a snigger, 'Ello?' she barely whispered, not daring to take another step. She took one tragic step and heard a sinister laugh. She took five small steps. She is now in the centre of the room. She gulps. 'You're gonna die in here,' a small childlike voice whispered. She jumped in shock. 'You're gonna regret it, you're gonna regret it,' the voice said over and over again, then... *bang!* Snow White was dead!

LAUREN KIRK
Davenant Foundation School, Loughton

Humpty Dumpty Had A Big Jump

Humpty Dumpty sat on a wall thinking of all the dead in their graves. Tossing and turning all about, a party they're having no doubt. The wall, quite high, offered to all and Humpty Dumpty thought that a jump could be a good end. Not a good life and no one to say, 'Humpty Dumpty, how good is this day?' And so should Humpty Dumpty jump this day? With no one to know or even to care Humpty Dumpty found peace. Elsewhere Humpty Dumpty stood on a wall. His grave was lonely.

Aaron Phillips (14)
Davenant Foundation School, Loughton

Sugar Sweet

Her eyes flashed green in delight. 'My children come here,' fangs dripping in children's tears. 'What a joy to have visitors.' The smell, a sweet smell of sugar and spice, a house made of candy,what a treat. 'Gravy or butter,' she chanted as she grasped the liquorice rope and bound her to the chair. 'Gravy or butter,' she repeated, 'Mmm butter it is.' She threw her into the oven, slammed shut the door and strode away. 'She got my brother but now I've got her.' There's a new boss in town. Blood will never run through the streets again.

Andrea Kriel (14)
Davenant Foundation School, Loughton

IS SHE ACTUALLY RAPUNZEL UNDER THAT WEAVE?

Once upon a time, there lived a young lady who had very long hair, her name was Rapunzel. But Rapunzel had a secret. As the story unfolds a hero comes to save her. The hero shouted out, 'Rapunzel, Rapunzel, let down your hair.' So she did, but as he was climbing up the hair he started to fall. Her weave had fallen out. He had it all in his hands. He suddenly looked, she had ten snakes coming from her head, they were as green as grass and their eyes were black as a night's sky. She was Medusa's sister.

HANNAH TURNER (14)
Davenant Foundation School, Loughton

THE DOG NEXT DOOR

I started barking at one o'clock. I woke everyone up with a sudden jolt. I felt happy when my mum came down the apples and pears. Then my mum said, 'Stop barking!'
So I said, 'No.' Then my owner came downstairs and let me go out to the loo. It was freezing cold for me so I did what I had to do! Yuck. When I got back inside I went to bed. The next morning I got up and went up the apples and pears to wake my owner and then I went out for a long walk.

MITCHELL WRIGHT
John Barker Centre, Ilford

OUTCAST!

No family, no friends, nowhere to go but the place my masters have called home. Sat on, cried on, sometimes even spat on. Have four legs but cannot move. I don't even have a clue! They clean me with burning acids! Trapped in a cage, imprisoned in no-man's-land. I cry in pain and sorrow, I cannot bear to live in such a horror. My life has no meaning but my life has no end. I never get fed. All I have is my price. They claim I am way above able but they just call me... Table.

PHILIP CHINWUBA (13)
John Barker Centre, Ilford

THE WOLF THAT CRIED HUMANS

Once upon a time there was a wolf that came to the hayfield and one day he wanted to trick his pack so he shouted, 'Humans, humans!' The whole pack came. They saw nothing so they left.
The next day he shouted, 'Humans, humans!' The entire pack came, then they left. One day he heard a boy shout, 'Wolf!' So he wanted to trick him. He ran to the boy and he screamed, so he ate him. Lots of humans came. The pack didn't bother to come after what he had done. Later that day the wolf was found dead.

JAWAD ISLAM
John Barker Centre, Ilford

DARK ALLEY

It was just after midnight... I was terrified. I didn't know who it was or what it was, but I knew for sure it was coming for me. I was alone. I could hear footsteps behind me. They were getting louder and louder but I just couldn't see who it was. I was horrified and trembling with fear. The dark shadows were getting bigger which meant it was getting closer. I began to run but the footsteps never stopped, neither did the shadows. Eventually I looked over my shoulder. My heart stopped. It was Tranele laughing his head off.

CHARLIE BEANY
John Barker Centre, Ilford

THE ROUND

The trigger pulled. I flew past the battle. Whizzing past soldiers as they tried desperately to keep their macabre demise at bay. The muddy field and gloomy scenery flew past me, a blur, as I bolted faster than once thought possible. I saw him. My target. A young man, freshly shipped from his home to this cruel, unforgiving war. Time seemed to slow, the movement around me, scenery moving at a crawl and an eerie silence in the air. Time became constant once more and there was impact. I hit. A crimson splatter sprayed from the man's chest.

JOE MITCHELL (15)
Poplar Education Unit, Rochford

Blood Red Roses

Seven dwarfs found a lost princess wandering in the woods. They took her home to their ivy-covered cottage with light beaming through the windows. She told them her evil stepmother wanted to kill her. They said, 'Stay inside the cottage, don't open the door.' But she opened the door to a witch, who gave her a poisoned apple. The princess took a bite and fell to the floor. When the witch left, she spat it out then cooked an apple pie for the dwarves. Now she has seven new flower beds in her cottage garden, which grow *blood red roses*.

Danielle Martin (12)
St Benedict's Catholic College, Colchester

The Ninjabread Man!

Once upon a time there was a man, he was called Terry. Terry was a baker by day and ninja by night. One winter's day Terry thought, *I want a companion to help me fight.* So Terry made a gingerbread man who had an icing sword and white chocolate armour. Terry and his ninja bread man became friends and fought against evil! The ninja bread man would go around and chop their feet off ready for Terry to come in and finish the baddies off. Over time the ninja bread man became brittle so Terry created a new friend!

Cieran Montgomery
St Benedict's Catholic College, Colchester

GOLDIBOB!

It was a sweltering summer's day and Goldibob's mum had sent him outside to get some fresh air. He thought he would go to the woods to play. Meanwhile deeper in the woods, three bears were going out. Their breakfast was too hot. While Goldibob was passing, he found their house and went in. There were three steaming bowls of porridge. He tried the first one, too lumpy. The second, too salty. The third, perfect! The bears were home, the door swung wide open and that was the gruesome, unfortunate end of dear, dear Goldibob. How sad.

OLIVIA FARRY
St Benedict's Catholic College, Colchester

THE BIG, BAD, LUCKY WOLF

The three little pigs each decided to build a house to keep them safe from the big, bad wolf. However, the wolf huffed and puffed and blew down the straw house of the first little pig and the stick house of the second pig. They took refuge in the brick house of the third little pig. The big, bad wolf could not blow down the brick house. However, the third little pig had not obtained planning permission. The local council ordered demolition and outsourced the contract to the wolf, who bulldozed the house and ate the three little pigs.

MAX CHILVER (12)
St Benedict's Catholic College, Colchester

DREADLOCKS AND THE THREE SCARES . . .

Once upon a time there was a young girl with dreadlocks draping down her spine. Her name was Dreadlocks, with three scares awaiting. One day Dreadlocks was walking down a winding road when suddenly a tall, slender ghost burst out of the old, rotten autumn bush. *Whatever,* thought Dreadlocks and carried on walking. 'Rawr!' Out jumped a rotten doll, which had scars all over her face, *OK, slightly odd,* thought Dreadlocks walking a bit faster. Dreadlocks was very scared and was now awaiting the next jump or attack. Nothing... yet anyway. Out jumped the most wanted murderer.

CIARA LUCY ROWE (12)
St Benedict's Catholic College, Colchester

THE HOUSE

It was a dark summer night in London where little Jimmy sat saying his prayers. He'd just said the final part when he spotted a light in one of the windows in the abandoned house across the road. His parents were asleep. He took his torch and set out across the tarmac towards the house. There was a mossy 'for sale' sign beside the crumbling wall around the dirty front garden. Jimmy opened the gate, walked down the path and opened the door. He walked in and went upstairs to the room where he saw the light. *Boom!*

TOM BROWN (12)
St Benedict's Catholic College, Colchester

THE THREE MURDEROUS PIGS

The smell of boiling bones filled the pigs' noses. There bubbling over the pot, the wolf's skin fell onto the floor. They all looked at each other with a gruesome face. Like a bullet from a gun, the pigs rushed over to the skin, tearing and chewing through it until there was no more. They repeated this many more times until there was no more. When they'd finished, the third pig looked out of the window to find a tall wolf looking through the window staring at the blood on their murdering hands. Was this the end of another wolf?

NIAMH HODGKINSON
St Benedict's Catholic College, Colchester

JACK AND KILL

Jack and Kill strutted up the hill looking back at the bloody corpses. Victims oozing out blood as knives were viciously dug into their poor, defenceless bodies. As they got to the top of the hill, staring soullessly at the old abandoned well, Kill thought about Jack and all he had done to him. Kill got sick and tired of Jack's attitude and decided it was enough. He clicked his neck with confidence, got his hands into position and pushed. Jack went tumbling down, breaking every bone in his body. Kill looked up with a grin from ear to ear.

JAY ALVAREZ
St Benedict's Catholic College, Colchester

SCAULDILOCKS AND THE THREE BEARS

Tiptoe. Tiptoe. Scauldilocks inched through the hallway with a smirk on her face and a branding iron in her hand. She started to feel hungry; hungry for blood! She emerged through the kitchen arch. Bloodshot eyes. Clenched fists. *Crash!* A bowl collided with the wall using unimaginable force. *Bang! Boosh!* Two more bowls struck the wall. Scauldilocks roared up the stairs without mercy. She confronted the bears. Papa Bear leapt in front of his family, but Scauldilocks had no sympathy. She burnt his heart, making him drop dead. Thereafter, no one knew what happened, although screams were heard for miles.

KATIE OWENS-DAVIES
St Benedict's Catholic College, Colchester

GRUMPLESTILTSKIN

In the town of O'Crumpleton a young maiden gave birth to a baby boy who she named Seth. When Seth turned seven the young maiden died very suddenly. Seth was alone. Until, one day, a grumpy man kidnapped him. His name was Grumplestiltskin. He raised Seth to be evil like him, but Seth always had some good in him. One day Seth escaped Grumplestiltskin's grasp and was never seen again. It was said that he deliberately stabbed himself to death so he would be reunited with his mother. He left a note so people would know about his tragic suicide.

MADDIE BARRELL (11)
St Benedict's Catholic College, Colchester

SUICINDERELLA

The noose and the beauty, standing on the chair. The silence of the house is what took her there. After years and years of slaving away for her sisters and her stepmother, she finally decided to stop. The ball is on but she isn't there. The prince will fall in love with someone else; this isn't how the story goes. She's supposed to be dancing the most important dance of her life but she isn't there! A wobble on the chair and she falls to the floor. Oh, wait, she was in the noose. Now there's just a dead beauty.

OWEN MORIARTY
St Benedict's Catholic College, Colchester

REDLOCKS AND THE THREE BEARS

Once there lived a greedy girl named Redlocks. Wandering through the woods, she spotted a cottage and decided to enter. Opening the door, she noticed three chairs beside a large table, with three bowls filled to the brim with steaming hot porridge. She jumped onto the smallest chair, began to devour the porridge. Immediately she turned green, then dropped to the floor. Suddenly three bears entered the cottage to find the little girl dead! Stepping over the girl, they sat down and began to eat. 'Ha, that will teach her not to eat bear berry porridge,' laughed the little bear.

NIAMH MARY O'NEILL (12)
St Benedict's Catholic College, Colchester

47

THE PERISHING PIPER

Once there was a town which had a problem – rats. They were everywhere. The problem was so big that the inhabitants would pay anyone fifty gold coins to get rid of them. Many came, all failed, then the Pied Piper appeared. He played his flute for days but the rats weren't going anywhere. When he was playing it was so bad that the people moved out until only he was left. 'Good that's done it. I have the whole place to myself.' He congratulated himself. But the rats had eaten all the food; the Pied Piper starved to death.

BANDI CSEREP (11)
St Benedict's Catholic College, Colchester

NOT SO GOODIE, GOODIE GOLDILOCKS

Bang! Goldilocks heard a gunshot, she knew it was her dad, he'd been out hunting. Goldilocks hated her dad hunting so she ran until her little legs couldn't carry her, into the forbidden forest. She ended deep into the forest finding a bloody rundown house. Goldilocks opened the door and a cloud of dust blew into her face. She stepped into the house seeing something horrifying. Goldilocks' dad had just shot three brown bears, they were only young. Goldilocks wanted to put a stop to it and before she knew it she'd shot her dad right in his hairy chest.

ANTON ALVAREZ
St Benedict's Catholic College, Colchester

The Possessed Killer

I push through the trees with no hesitation. I'm running. I'm running from my certain death. The silhouettes of the towering trees dominate the lush forest. Rain viciously bellows down from the heavens above, setting the scene for this ominous occasion. This forest seems never-ending! The wind howls. I trip. Lightning flashes, causing me to see my killer for the first and final time. I'm in distress at what I learn; my killer is… my late sister! The stagnant odour of decomposing leaves disgusts me. She retorts, 'Your time has ended!' as I draw my last breath.

TEMI ADEPOJU (12)
St Benedict's Catholic College, Colchester

Hoodwinked

In an overgrown forest, a red hooded girl appeared. Along the path she wailed. *Crunch, crack, crunch, crack,* footsteps sounded. In front of her deep shadowed face, a wolf emerged. She carried on not caring about what she saw. From a twisty, curvy tree a skeletal man hung; she walked on still not caring. An imposing man disguised. Scared now; keeping still, shivering she crept backwards, not looking where she was going. 'Ahhhhh, my leg! Help, help!' Shape-shifting wolf-man and girl. Yelps of recognition. Daddy.

AMAIA D'SOUZA (11)
St Benedict's Catholic College, Colchester

MURDERELLA

So, Cinderella. She's a slave and then finds her Prince Charming. This is all wonderful and she may be told to be a lovely girl, but this is the truth... She was actually... a murderer... She was a power-hungry troublemaker. She killed her own husband so that she was the richest. She had all the power. But why did she stay with her stepmum if she was a murderer? That's all fake. She forced her horrible stepmum to buy her a beautiful ballgown and a diamond-encrusted coach. No godmother involved. Cinderella is a murderer.

ANNIE SALTHOUSE (11)
St Benedict's Catholic College, Colchester

THINK BEFORE YOU INK

Bluebell Blue, a new pupil, displeased Serena Sentence, the house captain, who was the best at writing poems. Mr Punctuation had always admired Serena until Bluebell arrived. As Bluebell's poem won the Poetopia competition, Serena fixed her pen to explode. Bluebell, blinded by the ink and with eyeballs bleeding, blundered into the nursery department where there were seven toddlers called Calpol, Tyxilix, Dummy, Thumb-Sucker, Non-Sleeper, Milk-Spewer and Giggler. They let Bluebell sleep on the floor mat but Serena came with a sponge of ink to wash her face. Luckily Wez Wally gave her wet wipes and they fell in love.

JACKIE CHEN (11)
St Benedict's Catholic College, Colchester

WHAT REALLY HAPPENED TO CINDERELLA AT THE BALL!

Cinderella was cleaning floors, commanded by her stepmother and stepsisters. There was a strange feeling in the house that day as it was the day of the ball and both sisters were excited, but Cinderella wasn't allowed to attend. After they left, the most surprising thing happened – a fairy godmother appeared, performed her magic but with only one flaw; Cinderella had to leave the ball at midnight. Cinderella didn't know why but she promised she would leave on time and at midnight she thought the magic would end, but instead the nightmare started. A bomb was detonated. Blood everywhere... Darkness!

ELLIE GIGER (12)
St Benedict's Catholic College, Colchester

UGLY AND THE BEAST

Once upon a time there lived an ugly girl named Belle. She was very mean and cared about no one but herself. One day she felt very mischievous, so she turned the prince into a beast. The prince spent ages plotting his revenge, excluded from the outside world. He finally decided to find her. When he did, he pleaded, 'Turn me back.'
'No,' she replied.
'Fine,' he said as he gobbled her up.

JESSICA EMILY STEBBING (12)
St Benedict's Catholic College, Colchester

Farm Boy

A young farm boy perched on a moss encrusted rock, supervising his sheep. Raindrops soaked his hair and dampened his clothes whilst he rocked back and forth. An eerie sensation tingled up his spine. Hairs on the back of his neck reached out for the warm atmosphere he could feel behind him. The image of a creature came to life in the puddle below him. Hairy arms outstretched in a contorted array; masses of spiky claws arranged to kill. 'Wolf!' he shrieked. The boy sprung to his feet and ran away, leaving the tree staring down at her reflection.

ABIGAIL MCNAUGHT (12)
St Benedict's Catholic College, Colchester

Knight In Shining Armour

I went to battle, decked in steel. Then my sword, I began to wield. I turned around to see a mace. It got me directly in the face. Next thing I remember I was on a fire. I knew the situation was very dire. My armour had melted into my skin. I would never see my next of kin. I took a deep breath and opened my mouth. Molten metal entered and now I'm a statue in someone's house.

PETER CONWAY (12)
St Benedict's Catholic College, Colchester

THE STRIKE

'Indeed, I must say this tea is quite nice!' said the snob poshly.
'Indeed, it's a...' *Boom!*
'Get down!' exclaimed one random burglar who was robbing The Ol'
Snobbies, which was a restaurant.
'Sir, may I...' *Bang!* The butler started bleeding, by a brass bullet, and
went. As you know it, all the snobs legged it!
'This may be a great robbery!'
'I must say, call the...' started the snob who was hiding under a table.
Eventually the police came, 30 minutes later, and arrested the snobs
for a hoax call. As they went, the robber was the butler.

JEREMY OZKAYA-SIMMS
St Benedict's Catholic College, Colchester

DINNER

Once upon a time there lived a lion who roamed the lands of the
Amazon jungle. His moral was eat, sleep, kill, repeat. He was the
greatest king of all lion kings, but what he didn't know was he was
being spied on by the Animafia, who were a group of crocodiles. One
evening, just as he fell asleep, the Animafia approached and stalked
the lion. They pounced, killing the king for the crocodiles to reign.
They tortured every other living animal so the crocodiles lived happily
ever after.

ELKAN BAGGOTT
St Benedict's Catholic College, Colchester

TRAILER TROUBLE

As I wandered down my shortcut on the way back to my home from the castle, a strange noise came from the abandoned trailer. Being ambitious I went to investigate. As I approached, a terrible groan echoed through the hallow shell of a building. Suddenly a green tinted villager jumped out at a snail's pace. It all happened so quickly, in a matter of seconds I was almost completely surrounded by zombies. If I was anyone else except myself, I would have not had the guts to chop off two of their limbs to get away.

FINLEY BRETT (12)
St Benedict's Catholic College, Colchester

DUCK LIFE

One day in the lonely fields of Devon, a farmer lived on his farm. He was looking for a love on Match. Out of the blue someone knocked on his door and shouted, 'There are ducks for sale.' So with his money he bought a flying duck. The next day he put his duck into a competition, he won!
Weeks later he won the Duck Championship. He went back to his house but to his surprise, gangsters were burning his farm. The gangsters saw him and pointed at him with a gun.

HARRISON SWATLAND (11)
St Benedict's Catholic College, Colchester

THE UNLUCKY NUMBER

It was Friday the 13th of July 1997 and England were playing Argentina. The game was half an hour in and suddenly it went all dark ... it was a solar eclipse. The game stopped, everyone looked, but as they looked a sudden flash occurred from out of nowhere. A player for Argentina was down, the number 13! All the players reported seeing a shadow run off into the night...

SEBASTIAN ALSTON (12)
St Benedict's Catholic College, Colchester

WHO'S AFRAID OF THE BIG, BAD WOLF?

The fairytale Little Red Riding Hood used to tell children to listen to their parents and not talk to strangers, but what really happened? And who is afraid of the big bad wolf? Is he really what he is portrayed to be? Did he really blow down the little pigs' houses and try to eat Little Red Riding Hood's grandmother? He died in both stories, surely he can't be killed twice? Can he? Was he framed, or did he just come back from the dead to cause chaos? What is the truth? The truth is, he never existed...

SHANNON REEDER (12)
St Benedict's Catholic College, Colchester

Happy Ever After . . . Really?

Over the land of princesses, the stench of death wafted in the air. Snow White's been pecked to death and Rapunzel's been strangled by her own hair. Sleeping Beauty drowned after being pushed into a lake by beavers, Belle's been killed by her father's machines, Anna was killed by Sven, who got jealous of her and Kristoff. Mulan turned into a man, went to battle and died. Pocahontas got eaten by a willow. Meanwhile, Tiana, in frog-form, was fried and eaten by a hungry Frenchman. Guess it wasn't really happily ever after, otherwise they would all still be alive.

Elizabeth Cooper (11)
St Benedict's Catholic College, Colchester

Cinderella

They teased, she found it funny... For a while. They called her Cinderella, it was funny... For a while. They kept on going and she tried to laugh it off, then the insults got worse! 'The only reason you took that apple was because you couldn't afford to buy one!' She never told anyone. Even her stepmother was awful to her, 'Go do the dishes, Ella!' When she told her father he didn't believe her. She became depressed.

Ebba Paterson (12)
St Benedict's Catholic College, Colchester

THE THREE GANGSTA GOATS GRUFF

It all started when they came. Everything fell apart, things were set on fire, innocent people were murdered and things were stolen. At first everyone suspected goblins, but we couldn't be more wrong... It was the three gangster goats gruff! They are not who you think they are. They are not sweet goats trying to pass over to the other meadow, they are vile murderers! First they shot poor troll and sent him off a cliff then they ate all of the other meadows resources. So you better lock away everything you own... Because they are here!

SHANNON PAYNE (12)
St Benedict's Catholic College, Colchester

RUMPEL 'STEAL YOUR SKIN'

On the outskirts of the village of Grimsdale there was a small hut, covered in skin! Inside was a stout, hunchbacked man by the name of Rumplestiltskin. What the villagers didn't know was those skins were human skins. He would settle on a likely target, stalk them and then when they went to sleep, pounce. It would be a flash of blades and the deed was done. Darkness fell, all was silent except the dark figure looming in the shadows. It opened a door, a woman screams. A blooded, skinless corpse on the bed. A new skin on the cabin.

BRADLEY ANDERSON-SMITH (12)
St Benedict's Catholic College, Colchester

CINDAKILLER

Cinderella walked into the ball with a small smirk on her face. She had a plan, to kill everyone royal at the ball and become queen. It has always been her dream so her it is. She lured the royal family and killed them. Then one by one the guests started disappearing and leaving their life. Her dream was coming true! She would finally be Queen! When suddenly someone came in, she was caught red handed and frozen to the ground. She was shot straight in the chest and right there and then Cinderella was killed by her own sister...

LAURA SZMAKOW (11)
St Benedict's Catholic College, Colchester

GERDA TRIUMPHS IN TRICKERY

Gerda peered through the curtain of rapidly plummeting snow. She smiled villainously to herself as she heard the mournful wail of her fading brother, Kai. Her trick had worked; the snow queen dead and her brother on the brink of death. The innocent people thought their queen had brought this monstrous winter. She cackled harshly. She would be hailed as a hero for saving the miserable town from a death from dense snow and wind. Kai couldn't get in her way, he had to die. She gazed once more into the snow, smiling with intense satisfaction as she ambled on.

INGE-MARIA C BOTHA (12)
St Benedict's Catholic College, Colchester

SNOW BLOOD AND THE SEVEN WOLVES

Once upon a nightmare there lived a devil dressed as an angel.
Thirsty for blood, she glared out the window of her castle dorm.
She was ready to call her seven wolves to slaughter everybody who
crossed her path. Her lips were red as blood and her eyes were dark
as the night's sky. The signal was made. Prepared to jump out the
window, she bid her hostage held stepmother farewell. The wolves
barked and the children screamed, the men tired to fight but she
was undefeated. An icy grin spread across her face, the witch, the
monster, Snow Blood.

LAURA SLACK (12) & ESME
St Benedict's Catholic College, Colchester

THE LAST PRINCESS

Locked up... in a bell tower.
Stuck... in chains of death.
Fear... crept into her mind.
Saw... gruesome things happening to her friends.
Smelt... of decay.
Heard... drops of blood dropping on the soggy floor.
Known... as the last princess ever to survive.
Called... Rapunzel.
Running away... from her life, soul and destiny.
Waiting... to reveal her secret...

ASCI CATABAY (12)
St Benedict's Catholic College, Colchester

THE UNIDENTIFIED STRANGER

One gloomy night in a forest, I went camping with my friends. We made a roaring campfire and pitched our tent. We were settled and comfortable.
The moon was up and the others were asleep. I was still awake, listening to incomprehensible noises. I couldn't see anything; the rest of nature was dead silent.
I quietly took my torch out, crept outside and scanned through the forest. All was still... The noises grew increasingly thunderous; my heart was beating rapidly. The seconds ticked by. Suddenly, something breezed behind my back. It whisked me away!

MATTHEW BARRY (12)
St Mark's West Essex Catholic School, Harlow

THE GORGEOUS LOOKING LADY

Every night when I cycle, I see a gorgeous looking lady gazing at the stars. One day the gorgeous looking lady invited me in. I was happy that she invited me in. I went in her room, all I saw was red. Red clothes, red bed, every single thing was red. Then I heard lots of clashing and banging. I got worried, I went to see the gorgeous looking lady. The gorgeous looking lady turned into a ghost. I realised she was going to take my soul. I tried to run but the doors were locked. My life was over!

ABEYSHAYKAA BALANDRA (13)
St Mark's West Essex Catholic School, Harlow

KINDER KILLER

She looked, then ran! Panting, I followed her little green coat.
The forest was dark and gloomy. She always use to sneak out to
come here! Hearing a high pitched scream I ran in the direction of
it, praying that my little girl was safe. I found her coat laying next
to a tall tree, then I held it in my arms. I heard voices. I walked
around the tree to spot my seven-year-old with her back to me, she
turned around. Her fangs pointed at the ground, like an arrow. She
pounced, then it all went black.

OLIVIA BURN (12)
St Mark's West Essex Catholic School, Harlow

WOOF!

It was around eleven pm when I walked my dog. I go round the
woods, through an alleyway, then back home. I was walking quickly
as it was raining. I heard a snipping noise and realised that the lead
had been cut, and my dog was gone. I looked around desperately
calling his name. Nothing, I started walking home, my eyes blurry
from crying. I completely forgot about what had cut his lead. I got to
my front door, only to find a man standing behind me.

JORDAN WASHINGTON (13)
St Mark's West Essex Catholic School, Harlow

HER

Arthur bit his lip. The door stood in front of him. He didn't want to go in, but the storm raged behind him and the bitter cold ate away at his flesh. The abandoned school was the only option. He walked in, instantly he regretted his choice. She stood in front of him, he blinked, she was gone. The door slammed, the lights flickered, the air thickened. Immediately he became tense. He could suddenly feel her warm breath on his neck. He cursed, he breathed in silently, his lost his breath. He stepped forward, his last step. He was gone.

TIA KELCHURE
St Mark's West Essex Catholic School, Harlow

MORE THAN JUST CANNIBALS

All I heard was the sound of squelching as I laid on the ground. Next to me stood tall trees and a smashed up car. I decided to investigate in hope of finding a living soul. As I got closer, it was clear there were at least three people crouching around a body. They weren't helping them, they were eating away at the flesh. Cannibals! A twig snapped, they saw me. I ran, but they were faster. They pulled me to the ground and it was clear they weren't just human cannibals, as they ripped into my fear riddled flesh.

AMARNI-JAI NEWMAN
St Mark's West Essex Catholic School, Harlow

RAPUNZEL

I wasn't going to do it, I swear, but then one of them said it. 'Rapunzel let down your hair.' I hate those five words with a passion, the number of times I've heard them is infinite. That's why I moved out here, in the hopes they'd never find me. They sought to chop off my locks, but of course I wasn't going to allow that. So I geared up, changed my image and that's how I ended up here in this predicament. Twenty slaughtered men at my feet and a crimson blade tied to the end of my braid.

LAUREN PITCHER
St Mark's West Essex Catholic School, Harlow

THE FINAL FEAST

Roaming the forest, covered in the blood of my last victim. I smelt it, the sweet, succulent blood of what would be my last prey. I could hear the blood pumping through her veins, I didn't want to hurt her, but I knew I would. I pushed off with every ounce of strength I had towards her. I bit her neck again and again, until she fell limp. Blinded by blood, I hadn't noticed him, staring down at me, my biggest threat, the vampire hunter. Before I knew it, I was on the ground, stake in my heart, dead!

HANNAH CARTER (13)
Shenfield High School, Brentwood

THE KILLING OF MALRAD ALASAD

17th June 2009 I was on a mission, operation Redwood, in the hills of Afghanistan making my way to Baghdad where I would kill Malrad Alasad. I was behind a rock, peering down into the valley, watching the town rip itself apart. Civilians being killed to stop spies to protect Alasad. Every ten minutes they would kill a few males, sometimes Alasad would come out. Then cracks of gunfire killing civilians in the valley. Then the wind stopped and I had my chance, looking down the scope, crosshairs at Alasad's head, *click*, *boom,* within a second, Alasad was dead!

WILLIAM SCOTT (13)
Shenfield High School, Brentwood

VICTIM

In 1772, he was made... A colour-changing slime ball that suffocates his victims. There is nothing anyone can do to stop the kill. This mutant sets out to destroy the adopted victim. In 1845, Martha was chosen. Her home was built in a dark, dingy forest. One dark night it trapped her, with no way out. *Crash!* The door swung open and a man appeared. He lurched forward rolling along the floor. The monster and the man struggled. Then silence! The mysterious man and monster to this day have never been seen again...

LUCY CRESWELL (13)
Shenfield High School, Brentwood

RECARNI, THE UNBEATABLE HELL DEMON

I felt his sting pierce my body and immediately the venom kicked in. Recarni, the demon. In his spider form, the size of an elephant, had succeeded. But as my body fell limp, it was not him who shrieked, but a woman's war cry. I came to, the pain from his sting, minor. Beside me was a woman, she looked bruised and cut. I realised she had saved my life, but how? 'I saved you from his venom with an antidote,' she said. 'However, he used his last ever sting on you, meaning you slew Recarni, the unbeatable hell demon.'

SOPHIA MORGAN (13)
Shenfield High School, Brentwood

THE PADDED ROOM

Most people are scared of ghosts, but not me. My name is Louise, I have a power. I see ghosts, that's why I'm under constant surveillance in a padded room. It started when I was just a baby. All I saw was transparent faces. As I grew up I would talk to them. My mother didn't understand, she thought that I had imaginary friends until I was seven. One day I was visited by the scariest, ugliest ghost I have ever seen. I screamed and ran to my mother, she made some phone calls and now I am here forever.

AMY TILLMAN (13)
Shenfield High School, Brentwood

THE PAINTER

'This one shall be appropriate...' It was 19th century London, at night it was cold, damp and thick with dew. He stalked an innocent young girl, with murder clouding his thoughts; he slit the girl's pretty throat. Without a sound he stored the fresh tantalising blood into a bucket and threw the limp corpse into the river. The next day he created a masterpiece, his painting stood proud for many years to come. Decades later, he was arrested on suspicion of a young girl's murder and was questioned on his identity. 'What is your name?' the inspector asked.
'It is...'

RYAN FLEMING (13)
Shenfield High School, Brentwood

UNNAMED KILLER

Bang! The door of the food delivery van closed to reveal an extraordinary young girl. 'This time tomorrow,' she said to the owner of the catering company and drove off, back to her apartment on the other side of town.
Walking down the alley, she stopped. There was a shadow behind her. A voice, rough and deadly, 'Don't move.' The girl turned to run but the large man grabbed her hair, but to his surprise he grabbed a wig. At her place there was a man with a cleaver, there was a short scream, then the deadly silence of night.

LEAH HUNTER (12)
Shenfield High School, Brentwood

Hell Beckons

Vampires hissing, werewolves howling, fairies deceiving their race and warlocks spilling energy. The common enemy awaits. Cheeks angular and bright, emerald eyes, his last words stood in Lily's brain, 'If Heaven shall not greet, I shall summon Hell'. That's what the demon did. *Fear rests inside you, don't let it control you*, she thought. With the creator at her feet, begging for mercy, Lily brought the blade down. A deep gurgle protruded from inside him, his motionless body slumped to the dust. Hell descended.

GRACE NOAKES (13)
Shenfield High School, Brentwood

Turning Point

The shewolf lived alone knowing her werewolf brother wasn't safe. He was possessed. She could recognise the stench of the zombie who gave her brother the crave for bloodshed that he had developed. She stumbled away. Chasing the zombie through the trees. She caught up to him and struck him. Death. As the shewolf arrived home, there stood her brother, he seemed clueless of what had happened to him over the past four years. She hugged him and he could hear her blood pumping heavily. He wanted to see it run. Screams filled the air. Her crimson blood satisfied him.

POPPY HASSAN (13)
Shenfield High School, Brentwood

THE DEADLY TRAIL!

There she stood, a little girl staring at evil, as he stared into her weeping eyes, blood dripped from his teeth. His skin pale and rotten. The girl ran holding her leg as it was dripping with blood, leaving an unwanted deadly trail. She's hiding now, but she can see him. Thirsty, he smelt her presence. Her heart beating out of her chest. He latched on to her, dragging her to the ground. *Thud!* Like a hammer against cloth, a scream that no one heard. He fled to the woods but it's not the end, yet...

MACAILA SMITH (15)
Tendring Enterprise Studio School, Clacton-On-Sea

THE RIDER IN BLACK

The man ran through the forest, you could hear nothing but the sound of running feet and trotting hooves. The man ran as fast as he could but it didn't seem to be enough. He knew not much of the man that was chasing him, he appeared to be headless. The man soon tripped over his own feet and stumbled down. The rider stood above him, carefully lining up his axe ready to finish. With one dreaded cut the man's life was ended. Just like the blowing out of a candle flame.

LEVI STANLEY (15)
Tendring Enterprise Studio School, Clacton-On-Sea

THE THREE LITTLE PIGS THAT DIDN'T LIVE

The pigs built their houses. The wolf came, the pigs hid in their houses. The wolf blew two down. The pigs hid in the brick house, but they forgot to shut the window. The wolf got in, then suddenly turned and ran. The pigs thought they were safe, they were wrong. For they were in danger of being eaten by something else, something worse. The pigs turned to see a big shadow casting over the room. The noise of drips hitting the floor, a big face with eyes as big as their house and razor sharp teeth.

CALVIN JAMES COOPER (16)
Tendring Enterprise Studio School, Clacton-On-Sea

THE SECRET OF ROBIN HOOD

The last thing he saw was an arrow, just before it landed between his eyes. Robin Hood, Nottingham's most notorious killer, struck again. Hood liked to torment the poor people of Nottingham by sending bits of his kill to the sheriff. People wondered if this murderer would ever be captured. Everyone sent to find him wound up dead or missing. The sheriff was desperate and needed a hero! Could a lowly man called Guy be the man who saved all of Nottingham from this vigilante gone rogue? No one suspected that lowly Guy was the true Robin Hood, for now...

CATHERINE DUNNE (17)
Tendring Enterprise Studio School, Clacton-On-Sea

The Red Hood

I was preparing to see my grandmother with some Chardonnay and bread. I put my red cloak around me and began my journey through the forest. On my way I grabbed a Big Mac meal, there are McDonald's everywhere. I met a wolf named Spurlock, he was a fat wolf. He said I should venture to JD and buy Grandmother some fresh threads. I agreed. As I arrived at the door it was open. I walked in, Grandmother's bed was empty and covered in red, a swift fur paw covered my face. A sharp pain engaged my body.

Paul Lawrence
Tendring Enterprise Studio School, Clacton-On-Sea

The Three Sizzling Pigs

Three little pigs arguing about sharing a house so they decided to built a house each. One pig made his house out of string, the second made his house out of plastic and the third made his house out of concrete. The wolf blew the house made out of string down and strangled the first pig to death. The wolf blew the second house down and cut the second pig in half. The wolf could not blow the third house down so he got a torch and burned it down and snapped the third pig's head off and ate him. The moral of the story: think before you act.

Daniel Brian James Cole (17)
Tendring Enterprise Studio School, Clacton-On-Sea

The Black Shuck

I felt so numb as I looked into the devils eyes, legends that i thought were only legends had proven to be real life. My blood ran cold and my heart beat increased, the Black Shuck stood just inches from me, looking at me... As if waiting, daring me to run but I couldn't. I was frozen in fear for the creature I'd read about for many years was just in sight and as terrifying as I once imagined. I closed my eyes waiting, only I opened them to see nothing. My eyes scanned the forest, the Shuck was gone.

Danni-Louise Cotier (16)
Tendring Enterprise Studio School, Clacton-On-Sea

The Night That's Not Forgotten!

The night was young. The smell of blood lingered in the air, tickling my nose as it passed. Fear building up inside of me. I entered my grandmother's house; which was now abandoned. Photos laying torn on the ground, which once captured such happy memories. Why did the wolf have to destroy my family? I walk in a little more to see the blood stained curtains from my grandmothers desperate attempts to free herself from the jaws of the evil beast. The memory will haunt my childhood, overriding all the good! I want revenge, it's what my grandmother deserves.

Shannon Readings (16)
Tendring Enterprise Studio School, Clacton-On Sea

Prince (Not So) Charming

She was a petite girl, lovely. A blonde girl, with a mission implanted into her brain, not worrying about the pain or the tears she caused, she didn't care. The voices told her to do it, the loud voices in her head. They went quiet. In fact they stopped, was she changing her mind? She went to the ball, looking beautiful. She ran out, the prince followed. Looked around for her, he noticed her shoe. Then she came crawling out of the bush, but it wasn't Cinderella, it was her mum. Her mum beheaded the prince very happily.

BETH MARIE BRIDGES (16)
Tendring Enterprise Studio School, Clacton-On-Sea

Three Little Donkeys And The Big Bad Meerkat

Once upon a time there were three little donkeys, their mother kicked them out. So they had to live by themselves but the first two didn't get a chance. The big bad meerkat beat and killed them but the first donkey ran and didn't look back. He built a big house and the big bad meerkat said, 'Let me in or I'll blow your house up.'
The donkey said, 'I will never let you in.' So the meerkat started shooting the bricks but he failed so he gave up and the donkey lived sadly after.

LIAM WILLIS (15)
Tendring Enterprise Studio School, Clacton-On-Sea

HANSEL ATE GRETEL

Two children called Hansel and Gretel were on the beach crying then suddenly they fell into a hole. They stood up and saw a big house made out of a roast dinner, they liked the gravy pool. A man told them to come in and he gave them lots of food, especially Gretel. He took Gretel into the kitchen and baked her into a pie and gave it to Hansel. Hansel ate it. He never knew, and Hansel and the old man lived happily ever after until the old man gets hungry, so watch out.

HONEY COLEMAN (12)
The Appleton School, Benfleet

THE DOWNFALL OF CINDERELLA

Blood trickled down her body and collects in a pool at the base of her feet. They drew the knife back and stabbed again. Crimson stained her gown. Her arms hung limp as life drains out of her. She slumps to the floor, just to be dragged back up by the chains binding her to the wall. The blade plunged back in, piercing another part of her porcelain white skin. Her eyes were closed as she seeped away, making the transition from life to death. With the last of her strength, she opened her eyes, just a squint. 'Hello Cinderella.'

REAGAN FURNEVEL (13)
The Appleton School, Benfleet

THE FALL

She was waiting to make her move… The blade in one hand and her hair in the other. 'Rapunzel!' he cried, 'let down your beautiful hair!' She was ready. 'Okay my darling.' Her hair flew down the tower, whilst the prince stretched his arms up ready to catch it. He was pulled up to the top of the tower. What he didn't know was that he was about to meet his death… Rapunzel leant in to kiss him – RIP! Her hair was gone and so was the prince. Her mother got back and saw him dead… 'What happened?'
'He fell…'

LAUREN THOMAS (11)
The Appleton School, Benfleet

POISON PORRIDGE

One day there lived a little girl named Blondilocks. She is twelve and has long hair in little plaits on each side of her head.
A few miles away lived three bears. Blondilocks would never go in there but one day she did. When she went inside she explored for a little while until she found three bowls of porridge. She tried two of the porridges and they were disgusting and there was one left, it was a tiny bowl of porridge. Blondilocks scoffed the entire bowl and a few minutes later she suddenly dropped to her death.

LUCY MARY-JANE PASK (11)
The Appleton School, Benfleet

SEVEN NIGHTS TO LIVE

Snow White arrived at a strange little cottage under a hill. When she entered the cottage, there were seven dwarfs. After staying there a week, she hated them! That's when she came up with her brilliant idea, to kill a dwarf each night.

The first night she killed Bashful by making him die of embarrassment. The second night she killed Dopey by telling him to drink a potion. She killed Doc by stabbing him. Happy by making him sad. She killed Sleepy by putting a sleeping spell on him. Sneezy by making him sneeze. Finally Grumpy by making him happy.

SIAN HAMBLETON (12)
The Appleton School, Benfleet

LITTLE RED CHAINSAW HOOD

Once there was a death hut and if you entered Little Red Riding Hood would kill you with a chainsaw. So one day on the 4th May 2001, she got told to take a basket of food to her Grandma. On her way she met a wolf who said, 'Hurry, hide, the government are on to you.' She just passed him and ignored him.

Through the woods, over logs, under branches, around trees, through gardens then she got to her Grandma's, but it was deserted. '3, 2, 1, fire the nuke.' *Boom!* Everyone died that day. The Earth now annihilated.

LAURENCE FARROW (13)
The Appleton School, Benfleet

Untitled

The little girl that has not been turned into a zombie had to go to her nan's. Red Riding Hood and the little girl walked out into the open and suddenly a zombie came out of nowhere and bit the little girl's neck. Red Riding Hood sprinted through the woods till she got to the bottom of the mountain. She looked behind her and tonnes of zombies dashed straight for Red Riding Hood. When she looked in front she saw a zombie. That was the last time we saw her.

Finley Huckfield (12)
The Appleton School, Benfleet

Untitled

The gentleman made his way in to see Beauty herself, lying on her bed of candles, she seemed so innocent compared to the monstrosity that killed her. He was shocked, he didn't know what happened. He made his way over to her bedside and lingered around for a little while, then leant in for a kiss. Suddenly, her eyes woke and she stole the dagger from his holster and pushed it into his chest. Maleficent was right, Beauty isn't as perfect as she seems.

Molly Kelly (13)
The Appleton School, Benfleet

LITTLE RED AND THE BIG WOLF

Once upon a time there was a little girl called Red. She was called Red because all she wore was red, her favourite colour was red, but back to the story. Red visited her granny every Sunday and took with her a homemade blueberry pie. Whilst she was heading to Granny's, through the woods, she was stopped by a big grey wolf. The wolf asked Red what she had in her basket. Red showed the wolf her homemade blueberry pie. The wolf sneakily put something in the pie, but Red didn't see, so she continued on her way to Granny's....

BRANDON LAWRENCE (13)
The Appleton School, Benfleet

JACK AND THE DARK STALK

A boy, Jack, bought some beans and planted them. One day later there was a black beanstalk. Jack liked adventures so he went up it, as he got higher up the stalk bats flew around him, they were circling Jack. Finally he got to the top of the dark beanstalk. At the top there was a sword on the floor, so he picked it up then suddenly a hydra jumped out so he stabbed its heart. Its blood was acid, then it went on the stalk and burned it down. Devastatingly, Jack was stuck up there forever!

JAMES LARKIN (13)
The Appleton School, Benfleet

LITTLE RED, HUNTED

As Little Red left Granny's to go home she realised it was dark. As she walked she heard howling but she could not see anything as there was a mist as thick as pea soup. There was a crunching sound getting closer, then stopped. Red's heart sank into her stomach as she felt breathing down her neck. She turned to see two glowing eyes staring. It emerged through the mist. 'Huntsman, I thought you were something out to hurt me.'
'Think again,' smirked Huntsman, with that Huntsman grabbed Red and ran off into the night never to be seen again.

EMILY NUNN (13)
The Appleton School, Benfleet

DANCE FLOOR MURDER

Cinderella danced for one amazing hour with the mysterious prince on the marbled floor. Their feet collided gracefully as the prince could see his reflection in Cinderella's crystal blue eyes. He smiled as the music stopped. 'This has been an amazing night,' he whispered. The music stopped and she held the prince's hand. 'I don't even know your name.' All of a sudden a huge group of people screamed, someone had been murdered. The prince began to sweat and ran letting go of Cinderella's hand and dodging plants down the palace steps, accidentally dropping his tie…

CHARLOTTE RANKIN (13)
The Appleton School, Benfleet

SNOW'S SECRET STEW

Snow was cleaning and cooking in the cosy cottage, waiting for her seven little friends to come home. As they approached, she put in the final ingredient for their dinner. One by one they walked through the door. They all sat around the table discussing how their day went, when they realised one was missing. Sneezy. Snow suggested he had probably gone to the market. 'Sit, eat, your dinner is getting cold, Sneezy can have his when he returns.' Snow smiled as she looked over at the dresser, with a bloody knife with Sneezy's hat sitting beside it.

AIMEE REVILL (13)
The Appleton School, Benfleet

JACK ON THE BEANSTALK

The old lady strolled away. She started to snigger as what Jack didn't know was that there was many side effects; growing into a fierce beast forever, he will live in a castle on top of a vast beanstalk. When Jack got home he ate the magical beans, he turned into a giant with arms as strong as a mansion. Jack then got transported to a huge castle made of bricks. All over the castle were plants overgrown with points. Jack terrorised the town for many years especially the very old lady.

GRACE TEDORE (13)
The Appleton School, Benfleet

WATCHER IN THE WOODS

The wind was high, blowing through the woods. He ran crashing through the leaves on the floor. No clue as to what it was. He got to the manor… he turned… there it was, looking right through him… the watcher in the woods.

BRADY WILSON-JONES (13)
The Appleton School, Benfleet

THE GHOST OF SLEEPING BEAUTY

The prince heard an awful sound coming from the door. He walked towards and opened the door. He saw nothing. When he turned around there it was: he recognised the face. It was Sleeping Beauty, but her hand was a weapon, it was a knife with blood on it. She said, 'I shall slice you up in pieces.' How could Sleeping Beauty do this when she was sleeping? It shows the devil side of her.
The prince didn't do anything, he was so scared. He said, 'What's that over there?' and then ran away. But Sleeping Beauty caught up…

AMY ROTHON (12)
The Appleton School, Benfleet

GOLDILOCKS

The young girl caught a sight. Over the hill. A little hut. The door slightly ajar. As she enters the finest porridge awaits her welcoming. As she begins to fiercely cram several spoonfuls into her mouth, she heard voices… with a quite intimidating tone to one of them, whereas another had a rather womanly tone, however, the last sounded like a little child, supposed to be a boy. As she proceeds to hide she notices three very inhuman figures; bears! Suddenly, one of them picks her up and slams her onto the table. Then one says, 'I found dinner!'

BILLY TAYLOR (12)
The Appleton School, Benfleet

BEAUTY THE BEAST!

The curse was broken. Beauty was scared, now she had to tell the prince her secret. 'I have accepted you for what you were now accept me for what I am!' she croaked. Suddenly, Beauty collapsed, breathing heavily, she was no longer a woman but a beautiful white wolf with piercing red eyes. 'I am a 'were' and you are my mate.' Immediately, the prince realised he wasn't the beast, she was and he was her mate!

NIMOFE WILSON-ADU
The Appleton School, Benfleet

THE SCREAM

The piercing scream was deafening from the woods. I crept slowly, worried what I would find! Twigs snapping under my feet was the only sound, my breath was short, awaiting my fate. I started to shake with fear, worried where the scream came from and what would happen to me. Out of nowhere appeared a little girl with her umbrella. Possessed without a doubt. How could I escape her gaze? She drifted towards me like a spirit. She was in my scared face. She gave me the death stare. I will never escape!

GRACE SULLIVAN (11)
The Appleton School, Benfleet

HANSEL AND GRETEL

Into the woods they walked, it was dark and gloomy. Scared. As they stumbled upon the well, a sudden crack of the bucket took them off guard. Out of nowhere, Gretel rose to the air. Gretel mumbled in a husky evil voice. Hansel ran with fear but tripped. Gretel appeared in front of him, picked him up, held him over the well and dropped him. She floated home and knocked on the door. Their 'mum' opened the door and looked at Gretel. Gretel stared back, glided in and baked her mum crisp…

KIERAN MCCOY (12)
The Appleton School, Benfleet

THE BIG FEARSOME GIANT

There was once a big fearsome giant who would go around snatching children. Once he had snatched a child, he would take them back to his den and boil them alive. No one has ever survived being snatched. Sometimes he would even take parents leaving children orphans. Those who went searching were never seen again. There are some who think that he is a god. They are the only people that have ever seen him and lived.

EVAN DAVID HUGHES (13)
The Appleton School, Benfleet

FROZEN . . . FOREVER!

As Belsa and Tanna were walking down to the pond, Belsa couldn't help but think about last night when, Belsa witnessed what looked like Tanna killing their cat, and sure the next day the cat wasn't around. 'Let it go,' she kept telling herself but she simply couldn't. So when they got down to the lake they could see the pond was frozen over. 'Let's just leave it,' and with that Tanna fell into the lake but Belsa just ran and left her to freeze. Tanna was struggling, screaming for Belsa, but she was gone. Tanna was frozen… forever.

WILL KEUNE (14)
The Appleton School, Benfleet

DEEP IN THE FOREST

Silence… A twig snapped, regret filled Nathaniel and the chase began. Through the forest he stumbled, his heart skipped yet another beat. Running, running was all he could think about. Running to save his life. His life, another thing he couldn't take his mind off, if he kept it, what would happen to him, if he lost it, what would happen to him? Wrestling himself through branches and crawling through trenches that he really thought were just made for this chase. The predator was ready to pounce, he knew he would win. He pounced. There was no hope now…

AMY ALLWRIGHT (11)
The Appleton School, Benfleet

THE VERY HUNGRY CHILDREN

Two children approached the gingerbread house, but they craved a different source of food. They noticed a witch covered in flesh, they look at each other and smiled with delight. They acted poor and pleaded for food, she ordered them inside, before a 'snack on the house'. She insisted they ate the wall and floor, it was gingerbread after all. She prepared an oven, fit for children, little did she know that their bloodthirstiness was stronger. She looked at them, and grinned, but she stared as they rushed towards her and devoured her alive.

CONNOR HOPKINS (14)
The Appleton School, Benfleet

LITTLE RED RIDING HOOD

Once upon a time there was a little girl who was going to her grandmother's house. She was on her way when a wolf came along behind her. Then at that moment, when the bloodthirsty wolf went to strike at the girl, she spun around and snapped the wolf's neck. The girl found a bottle, scooped up the blood, took the teeth and put them in the bottle for dinner later. That girl's dress was white but the wolf's blood that came out of the wolf made her dress red.

MAX HALLETT (13)
The Appleton School, Benfleet

MYSTERIOUS MURDER

The adrenaline rushing through her was incomparable. The blood she saw, running down her friend's indescribable face. Crooked, struck by the force of the wind. The sight of her jawbone seized her lack of oxygen. Her kneecap twisted, turned. She finally expressed her revulsion upon her violent death. Now, becoming the same as her friend, like gazing in a mirror, she wondered how he was going to hurt her. Unthinkable. Strolling casually toward her, knife in one hand, whip in the other, all of a sudden he… 'Argh!'

LUKE McCOY (12)
The Appleton School, Benfleet

BEAUTY AND THE ROSE

I saw the castle, I knocked on the door. 'You're not safe here!' they said. They were enormous with scared faces.
'Please can I stay, I have nowhere else to go,' I shouted over the pouring rain. They let me in and my dress was soaking. I went upstairs and found a room with a rose in it.
'That's master's rose!' I turned round. 'My name is Chip,' he said. 'My name is Belle,' I said. I touched the rose and my legs turned to stone. 'What?' I shouted.
'You touched the rose, you're one of us now,' he said.

MEGAN EVANS (11)
The Appleton School, Benfleet

THE VICIOUS BEAST!

He looked at me with fear in his eyes. His big bushy hair spiked up on his neck. I thought to myself, *why, why me? What have I done?* I took a step closer to the beast who I thought I would be afraid of… turns out not. He growled at me with his spiky, vicious teeth. What was happening? I couldn't risk anything more. I turned away and ran to the guards but that first step was the worst mistake of my life. The beast turned around and ripped my head off. We were both never seen again…

OLIVIA LAMBERT (12)
The Appleton School, Benfleet

CINDERELLA FOREVER ... KIND OF

Horses pulling the pumpkin up the hill towards the grand ball. *Boom!* There was a sound in the distance. *Plop!* There was a sound close by – a head landing on the floor in fact. *Boom!* Another sound, but this time it was Cinderella, her head flying up in the air, a shower of blood and puddles of guts fill the streets. I don't think she will ever meet her love at first sight. Maybe she will one day in Heaven. Cinderella forever… kind of.

AMY FROST (12)
The Appleton School, Benfleet

SNOWY WHITE

Snowy smelt a sign of fear. Her heart pumped more than her leg pulse as she sprinted into the enchanted woods. She wanted her heart more than anything. Barging into the house not knowing what to do. She met the outlaw dwarfs, welcoming her to their home. Begging Snowy to get her kingdom back. They leave for supper but only a scream was heard. The beloved dwarfs ran but red dripping on Grumpy's boots. Snowy, never seen again, but left on cold grey stone as cold as ice.

PHOEBE ELLIS (11)
The Appleton School, Benfleet

Blood Porridge

As the beast left their cottage, a young girl emerged from the undergrowth in the dark forest. The cottage was submerged under a thick layer of debris that the girl had to rummage through to get into the cottage. As she approached the crumbling pile the door became visible and accessible. She entered to be greeted by a room painted in thick red blood. The oak floorboards screamed as the girl paced the downstairs with confusion. She stared at three steamy bowls of porridge – each blood red with organs hanging, either side. Suddenly, huge claws decapitated her, shoulder to shoulder.

Cameron Gray (11)
The Appleton School, Benfleet

Haribo Saves The Day

There it was. The hay laying on the floor. Porky was hungry. He told Haribo to fry Gelatine so he could eat Bacon. He did so. After eating their own friend they were down to two. Suddenly, the wolf approached them. Porky was known for his strength and power. At one hundred miles an hour Porky chased the wolf. But, Wolf resisted Porky and ran off with his head. Within seconds, Haribo charged at the wolf. He started screaming, in a high-pitched voice. This defeated the wolf. 'Who's next?' screamed Haribo. As you can see nobody messes with Haribo…

Lionel Bones (12)
The Appleton School, Benfleet

THE THREE LITTLE PIGS GONE WRONG

Once upon a time there lived three pigs. They were playing when they decided to build three houses. They went to find materials to build their houses. The youngest pig found some straw, the middle pig found some twigs, the eldest pig found some bricks. Once the houses were built Mr Wolf had seen the pigs. The pigs hid from Wolfy but the wolf went after them and started to blow. *Crash!* The wolf blew the houses down but he forgot that the pigs were inside, they had been squashed by their houses so Wolfy couldn't eat them after all.

JOSEPH FROST (12)
The Appleton School, Benfleet

THE THREE LITTLE GRAVESTONES

The other houses weren't finished, so now all that's left in this story are three little pigs and one big house. The wolf couldn't blow it down so climbed onto the roof. The pigs heard scattering and knew that the only way in was the chimney, so they began to try and light a fire. They finally found the matches but struggled to light a fire. When the wolf jumped down they realised their plan hadn't worked.
So... Humpty Dumpty had a great fall and Little Bo Beep lost her sheep, but those three little pigs were never seen again.

CONNOR LATORRE-DOUGLAS (11)
The Appleton School, Benfleet

SNOW WHITE

Snow White, a beautiful young girl, her long black hair against her pale white skin, running through the woods, as she stopped running she came to a cabin. The door was rusty. She went inside. The floorboards creaked. She sat down on the bed, she heard a noise. Then a shadow. There was a loud bang. After a while Snow White woke up tied to the bed by her hands and feet. The seven shadows came to eyesight. One by one each of them grabbed a knife. Blood pools were everywhere.

MIA ROSE SPICER (12)
The Appleton School, Benfleet

THE WITCH'S TALE

There they stood. A series of traps beneath their feet, as they were unaware of who or what the witch was. There was a deep, dark silence. Unaware, they crept towards the traps, full or cunning and most importantly death. All of this was for the witch to have her ten thousandth human feast. Such was her insatiable need to consume human flesh, dripping from the bones, roasted, boiled, baked or simply rotting away. Still unsure to tread the next step, they moved further towards their fate. Step… *Crack!* went the undergrowth. Step… *Bang…* 'Argh!' they screamed, then total silence…

ANDREW MIDSON (12)
The Appleton School, Benfleet

LIGHTS OUT

10pm. Jane had got a drink and was walking back to her room. She turned the lights off. There! A woman! Jane turned them back on. Nothing was there. So she turned them off. There again, a woman! Quickly she turned them on. Nothing! Just an empty hallway. This time she left them on and hopped into bed. She closed her eyes when… *click!* Someone turned the lights out! Frightened she hid under her duvet. Who was it?
Thirty seconds later she slowly popped her head out. Nothing. Then the voice of a girl behind her said, 'Lights out!'

THOMAS WILLIAMS (12)
The Appleton School, Benfleet

CINDERELLA

Dancing Cinderella and Prince Charming. It turns 11.55. She runs as fast as she can. It's the third night of the ball. Once she gets to the stairs Prince Charming has trapped her, she escapes, but only with one shoe.
The next day, Prince Charming arrives at Cinderella's house. At first the eldest sister tries on the shoe, but it doesn't fit, so her mother cuts off her toe. Secondly, the next sister tries it on, but it doesn't fit therefore, her mother cuts off her heel. Then it was Cinderella's turn, it fit so she lived happily ever after.

DEMI ROBINSON (12)
The Appleton School, Benfleet

Is It The Scarecrow?

On a hill was a scarecrow, a symbol of a horrible man, John Scarecrow. One night was a storm and a flash of lightning hit the symbol and it came alive. Every night people tell the tale of John. After they told the tale they were never seen again. People say they ran away, others say that the scarecrow murdered them and it is true. Although it is made out of stuffing it can still eat bodies to morph into a flesh-eating person. So at night, lock your doors and windows, although there's no point, it will still come.

Bonnie Roth (11)
The Appleton School, Benfleet

The Story Of The Twisted Goldie

The three bears woke up to the fresh smell of Nando's but it was too hot so they went for a walk. Then twisted Goldy came through the door as they left, wiping her lips as she saw the food. Walking towards the table then she snapped and the food was gone. Then she stormed up the stairs and hid under the beds, waiting for the bears to arrive. And then they appeared and screamed, 'Where's my food?' They strolled up the stairs and got ambushed by the twisted Goldy and then *boom!* The bears lay dead.

Jayden Wicker (13)
The Appleton School, Benfleet

THE THREE LITTLE PIGS GONE WRONG!

As the day turned to night, Wolf was getting tired, but he was not giving up, this brick house was not defeating him this time... He returned with a chainsaw later that night ready for his bacon dinner. One wrong move from the little pigs and they knew they were dead meat. Wolf burst through the weak, wooden door, chainsaw ready to kill. The pigs backed into a corner, shivering, scared for their lives. Wolf gave power to the chainsaw making the roar as if it was angry. The littlest pig snuck behind Wolf and stole the chainsaw. Goodbye Wolf...

EVIE DUGGAN (11)
The Appleton School, Benfleet

A LIVING NIGHTMARE

As darkness descended across the blood wrecked land, a gruesome creature appeared outside Lola's door. He had shining red skin and a repulsive stench. Petrified, Lola ran, hiding in her oak wardrobe. He entered, stopping outside where Lola was hiding. He sniffed, could he smell her fear? As shock rushed down her spine like a waterfall, Lola ran out of her room. Suddenly, he let out a horrible scream. It was a sound that ripped a nightmare into reality. She was safe... for now...

ABIGAIL LOMAN (12)
The Appleton School, Benfleet

Blood Red

Snow White felt power rushing through her veins. Her previous good life had been wiped away like a dream. Silently, she sat up and looked at her 'prince'. With a single slice of glass across his face, he fell down. Dead. Her face pale and her dress torn from the terrors of yesterday, she left her coffin. She walked towards her evil stepmother. 'I don't know what you put in the apple, but it worked,' Snow White said. Together, they walked through the forest with an evil look in their eyes.

Georgie Musson (12)
The Appleton School, Benfleet

Snow Fright

She walked down the winding stairs to find the seven dwarfs sitting at the table eating. Their pointy hats and little legs had worn thin on her, she hated them. If she told them she would spend life in prison as she was a good queen, instead she decided to kill them.
That night, before dinner, she glossed up her red lips and combed back her black silky hair. She grabbed the poison from a drawer and added a drop to all of the dwarfs' food. Slowly one by one the dwarfs fell into a deep, deep sleep forever.

Holly Howes (12)
The Appleton School, Benfleet

The Predator Of The Woods!

Rumble, rumble, she turned around, she saw nothing. Her red cloak scraped the floor as she walked home. Louder and louder the rumble became, her heart was pounding, faster than her footsteps. Something was gaining on her, she didn't know. *Roar!* It growled but it wasn't the rustler, it was someone else. She ran and ran as fast as she could, the predator gained. His teeth were visible. She tripped and fell. The wolf waited for her to look up. She turned round and the wolf fell, he'd been taken down by the evil panda, predator of the woods.

KATIE NUDING (11)
The Appleton School, Benfleet

Glass (The Little Mermaid)

It hurt every time she took a step. The shards of glass making themselves comfortable inside her foot. That was the consequence. Fire controlled her. The deal that she had made, to be with the one she loved. The poison she had inhaled, just to be with the one she loved. Darkness and fear controlled her every movement. Shadows followed her. The pain has to stop. To sacrifice her life, for her one true love. She was gone, because of the voices inside her head. It was over.

REBECCA GILLETT-JONES (12)
The Appleton School, Benfleet

THE WOODS

Awoken from their last night of misery, Hansel and Gretel, seek through the woods. Suddenly, a rustle from the trees shakes the children. A mysterious creature emerges from the withered trees, cautiously moves towards the children. A tall male with hazel eyes, hair spiky like thorns on a rose and hair red as a rose. From head to toe this monster is dressed immaculately. Fur smooth as silk and voice deep and heavy. Without a blink of an eye, Gretel pulls a blade out and injects it into the monster's heart, he stumbles to the ground to a miserable death.

BRIANNA LAWAL
The Appleton School, Benfleet

THE UNDEAD

Once deep in the old forest there was a cottage with a baby in it, on a rocking chair singing lala, lala. The parents were out hunting, suddenly the baby crawled through the woods till it came upon a graveyard. It walked to the end of it but zombies started to rise from the ground. They pulled the baby apart and upgraded themselves. The parents returned and found the zombies dead in the porch.

SAM MORGAN (11)
The Appleton School, Benfleet

THE FAMILY OF WOLVES

Three wolves, three pigs, how easy will this be? Take on a pig's house and we will have tea! The straw house let Wolf One in. 'A biscuit for you Sir.' The wolf munched until he dropped down dead, poisoned! The wooden house next and Pig offered Wolf Two a seat. With silent trotters he crept behind and used his iron on his head. The brick house had an open door so in walked Wolf Three. With blade in hand, out jumped the pig and Wolf was crumpled to the floor. Never trust strangers, no matter how small they are.

ALEX BOORMAN (11)
The Appleton School, Benfleet

THE MAN IN BLACK

There was a man. Everything on him was black. He even painted his skin black. One day, he was talking to his team member about murdering someone, 'I'm going to murder someone,' he said. They discussed the topic for a while. Eventually, the man in black said to his team member, 'Do you want to know who will be murdered?'
'Who?' said the team member.
'You!' said the man in black.

BENJAMIN HAMILTON (12)
The Appleton School, Benfleet

FEAR

Your fear, he can smell it. He's coming closer. You're alone now; he knows you're alone. He edges closer. Even as you're reading this very story, he's there. You don't realise he's there but he is. You're making yourself vulnerable. He is coming for you. You can't see him, although he can definitely see you. He smells your fear, your frantic decisions amuse him, you can run, you can lock yourself away from the world, but that's what he wants. You're amusing him, he's closer than ever before. Are you ready? You are vulnerable and now he has got you.

DAISY LOUISE HILL (12)
The Appleton School, Benfleet

UNTITLED

'Help!' she screamed. In the corridor, desperate to get away. We stood and ran, terrified, to the door. She screamed again, but stopped. The teacher in front of us ran into the corridor. She froze, horrified, then fell. I slowly began walking towards her, knowing I shouldn't. The teacher was now in front of me, motionless. My heart was thudding so loudly I couldn't hear. I closed my eyes and turned towards it. I opened them quickly. The screaming girl was laying by the corner of the corridor. Next to her it was there, staring into my eyes, oh no.

MIA FIELD (13)
The Appleton School, Benfleet

CINDERELLA AND THE 'IT'!

The moon shining down on the lake. Cinders stumbling up the charcoal covered path. When she finally arrives at the dark mansion, the prince was waiting. Cinderella was suspicious. What was up with the prince?

Two hours had gone. No one had stayed at the party, why? In the distance a tall shadow crossed over the staircase. Was it a ghost or was it the prince? Searching, Cinderella found the prince, but not the prince as she knew him. Prince Frankenstein. 'Argh,' was the last noise heard. Cinders was never seen again. The prince had taken Cinders' life away forever.

LUCY JAYNE JESSEP (13)
The Appleton School, Benfleet

DANGER

Knock, knock, knock. A steady sound was coming from the room next door. Muddy footprints led from the front door. I followed them. I came across a block of wood and grabbed it. The footprints led to the bedroom. Quietly but slowly, I opened the door. I heard a sudden noise, I walked over to the cabinet and gently lifted the lid. My head turned and looked straight at it. There it was. A short fat thing. 'Argh!' I screamed. Slowly I stepped back. He followed. I turned around and fell to the floor. The creature stabbed my arm.

CHELSEA HUXTABLE (14)
The Appleton School, Benfleet

THE DEADLY BEAST

It was a dark stormy night in an old abandoned house where two girls hid. It was deep, deep into the forest away from the deadly beast. Their father set off hunting for the beast but never returned. So they thought it was their time to try and kill the beast. They made a plan of what they were going to do. On the important day the girls got revenge and the town got victory. The deadly beast never returned again.

NIAMH DINGWALL (11)
The Appleton School, Benfleet

WATCHING

Someone, somewhere, is watching you. They have always done so, and will always do so, until you depart from this world. They are your worst nightmare, your biggest fear. They lurk in the shadows, waiting. They are the person behind you on a deserted street. They are silent, merely a whisper on the wind. You never know that the person is watching you and you will never know who they are. Not until the last minute, the last second, when they pounce.

KATE SOUTHAM (15)
The Appleton School, Benfleet

RESURRECTION OF DARK MAGIC

A number of miles away from Hogwarts, a group of people in black robes stood around a black tomb covered in complicated symbols. They slowly lifted up their wands and they muttered a long string of words. A tremor moved swiftly through the earth. A shaking white hand moved the lid to reveal a purple cape. A ghostly, pale face stared at the dark night. The dead body of the darkest wizard rose, very much alive, again.

JESPER WONG (11)
The Appleton School, Benfleet

UNTITLED

Once upon a time lived a girl called Cinderella, she lived with her stepmother and stepsisters, they kept her in a dungeon. She had to eat rare maggots that made her violently vomit. The stepsisters and stepmother were dressed in black because they were on their way to the kingdom called Die, Die Ville for the funeral of the king, but who killed him?
On the way there the horse and carriage stopped! The stepmother got out, suddenly there was a dark mysterious figure standing in the dark forest. Suddenly, she ripped out the figure's heart but who is he?

LEAH HASLER
The Appleton School, Benfleet

A Wolf's Mistake

The pigs in the brick house were petrified as the wolf followed behind, ready to make their insides their outsides. From two of the pigs last encounters, they knew the wolf would try and blow the house down. One pig had an idea. As the wolf was climbing the house; the pigs were making a trap. The pigs waited for the wolf to get to the chimney. As the wolf came down the chimney he landed in a huge bowl of boiling water and disintegrated and let out a painfully long howl.

Joe Turner (12)
The Appleton School, Benfleet

The Hot Light

The wolf got to the last house that was brick, he had no chance blowing it down, he will have to use a tank or something powerful. He saw a big chimney on the roof, so he climbed up the brick house and made his way to the chimney. Then he jumped down the dark, dusty, tight spaced chimney. He noticed it was getting warmer the deeper he got. He saw what he thought was light so he jumped down. He burnt to death. It was lava not light. No more Mr Wolf.

Ben Matthews (13)
The Appleton School, Benfleet

Untitled

The old bloodthirsty witch saw her prey standing outside of her gigantic sugar coated house. She waited until the perfect moment to grab them. She started to set everything up: the gigantic cage to keep them held hostage and to fatten them up for the oven to cook them. But little did the old lady know that as she walked outside into the dark forest to lead Hansel and Gretel inside, they had disappeared. She wasn't the only trickster around her in the eye-blinding woods.

JAMES LUKE GOWENS (13)
The Appleton School, Benfleet

Three Evil Pigs

The disturbed wolf got closer and closer to the brick house, he knew blowing it down would not work, if he wanted dinner he had to get in there. Out the corner of his eye, he saw it, silently he climbed up the chimney, he had no time to look down, he just flew into the chimney shouting, 'Surprise!'
Seconds later, he was stuck in a pot of fire as the pigs let out a mighty evil roar while the poor old wolf was burning to death.

JOSEPH PETTITT (13)
The Appleton School, Benfleet

UNTITLED

He saw them, he saw them through the window. Three tasty pigs sitting around the fire. What the wolf would do to cook them, he would do anything. So he did. He climbed onto the roof of the brick house to find a way in but there was only one way: the chimney. He jumped. He went face to face with the pigs. The wolf grabbed one of the pigs, that was a mistake. The two pigs knocked the wolf out. The wolf woke up later that day locked up in a cell where nobody could hear his screams.

TOBY STEPHENS (13)
The Appleton School, Benfleet

BABY BEAR'S ACCIDENT

Silence, all Baby Bear heard was silence. He crawled past the shattered bowls to find his one not shattered but empty. Baby Bear was petrified about the vandalism, therefore he went to sit down; once again Baby Bear discovered two shattered chairs and his chair not shattered but used, suddenly Daddy Bear heard snoring from upstairs – he was fuming. He stormed upstairs, he saw a girl on Baby's bed, she had elongated, golden locks. As Daddy opened his mouth you could see his glistening razor-sharp teeth, he let out a colossal roar! She was never seen again.

MAX O'BRIEN (12)
The Appleton School, Benfleet

UNTITLED

His belly grumbled! He knew it was time. He ran to the small cottage in the middle of the woods, he knew that he had to eat Grandma first and then wait for Little Red Riding Hood. He burst open the door but something wasn't right, Grandma wasn't in bed. He checked the house three times but Grandma wasn't there. So he decided to just go home, but as he walked out she was standing there with an axe. The wolf ran! Later that night, Grandma and Little Red Riding Hood, were sitting comfortably on their new wolf skin rug.

LOUISE KING (12)
The Appleton School, Benfleet

THE WITCH

She had just finished eating one batch as she heard more! She could not decide what to do. Her hunger for more took over her. Silently staring she let them eat before the big meal! She welcomed them. Their reaction was of shock and surprise! They immediately apologised! She trapped them with fear. Gone to get ingredients, they disappeared! She had enragement running through her veins and she was now in despair! Her stomach wanted more. She found no more. She could not stand much longer until she was no more.

FABIO ALMEIDA (12)
The Appleton School, Benfleet

UNTITLED

The three bears had just gone out to do the shopping, and they had left the door open. Goldilocks, being a menace, went into the house. She saw three bowls of porridge on the table, there was a big bowl, a medium bowl and a small bowl. She tried some from the big bowl, she didn't like it. So she had a mouthful from the medium bowl, she hated that more than the first one. Finally she took a spoonful of porridge from the small bowl, said it was just right, she finished the porridge and left.

RILEY HOLLAND (13)
The Appleton School, Benfleet

STARVED FOR SECONDS . . .

He was starved. He waited until the perfect moment for his prey, nobody came along; he had to search, not caring about anybody else, he ran through the woods hunting down his prey, but here, a very unusual looking cottage came into view. He slowly crept up to the door, and knocked. A very old grandma opened the door, he smelt fear, she smelt a starved wolf. She cried. He grinned. The grandma knew she was going to be his dinner and she tried to rush past him but she would never ever, ever escape. Was this the end…?

IZABELLA LACEY (12)
The Appleton School, Benfleet

UNTITLED

They were ravenous; their porridge still hadn't cooled down. Walking through the house they realised they had a visitor, but she wasn't going to stay for long. Knowing as soon as the visitor sees, she would flee, they crept up the creaky stairs. They didn't care who she was, they wanted her gone. Together they lifted up the covers. She awoke. The bears roared, she sat there confused. Laughing, she stood on the bed. 'Boo!' she whispered with eyes growing red. The bears bolted out of the house as fast as they could, would they ever come back?

CHLOE HOLMES (12)
The Appleton School, Benfleet

UNTITLED

The wolf caught a glimpse of the pink, plump pigs but as they saw his blood-red eyes, they ran! Building houses were the three intelligent pigs, well one was anyway, one house of straw, one of sticks and one of bricks. The first two pigs were easy to catch but the third pig was too smart. The wolf realised he couldn't blow this house down so he climbed down the chimney but that was the end of his reign of terror as the three little pigs ended his life for good.

FINLEY LLOYD (12)
The Appleton School, Benfleet

Don't Dream In The Forest

The ferocious wolf, who was starving, edged in on the vulnerable grandmother with his vicious teeth at the ready to eat her whole. Then, the wolf was the only living thing in the cottage. *Bang!* The door was bust open by a mysterious figure coated in a ruby-red cloak. The wolf got so scared that he ran out the door faster than a cheetah. He tripped over a branch that was sticking out the ground. The wolf felt glad that it was a dream, because otherwise he wouldn't be very brave at all.

Lewis Crickmar (12)
The Appleton School, Benfleet

The Wolf!

Two targets down; one to go! He was the top predator, and he was making his mark. The first victim was the easiest with poor results; all the animals tried to build their defences. Fat pig no 1 was first! He constructed his house out of straw (which didn't last long). Fat pig no 2 constructed his out of wood (which didn't last long either). Fat pig no 3 was in sight, however his defences were made of brick. He couldn't get in. He tried the chimney but he got burnt. This top predator has just become the frightened pony.

Callum Highfield (13)
The Appleton School, Benfleet

MISSING

It was just an ordinary day, but as you can tell something went wrong. I was in my room doing what I usually did, texting my friends, when I heard something. I crept down the stairs as quietly as I could and peered into the living room. I saw something glinting on the stairs; I bent down to pick it up. My finger started to bleed. It was glass. I ran into the room. I knew something had happened. Unconscious on the floor was my dad. My mum was missing. I never saw her again.

SUMIYA AHMED (12)
The Appleton School, Benfleet

JUST A WALK IN THE WOODS

The crooked witch was hiding in a tree when she heard a laugh. Two children. Lost and confused; perfect for a meal. She had seen her prey and was determined to get it. The witch waited for them to pass then pounced on them like a predator. She grabbed them, silenced them and pulled them to her sugar house like toys. The witch stood them on stools, tied ropes around their tiny necks, tied together their helpless hands, wiped their selfless smile from their faces, and let the stool free. This is a story that doesn't have a happy ending.

LIBERTY POWELL (12)
The Apploton School, Benfleet

IMPATIENCE CAN KILL

The wolf saw it. That pale skin which he would devour within a minute. There it was again. The wolf had no patience anymore. He ran through the prickly bushes ignoring the pain that was growing in his feet. He could almost reach out to grab the wonderful pink prey but something caught him by the ankle. He fell to the floor, hitting his head on a stray tree stump. The wolf sat up on his elbows to look at whatever had stopped him. There wasn't anyone there; apart from his pink coloured dinner. His prey smiled. 'Not this time.'

CHLOE GIBBS (13)
The Appleton School, Benfleet

THE CHASE

Dumbledore hastily trudged through the undergrowth. The moonlight glooming through the withered trees, staring into his soul. Dumbledore suddenly froze as the crackling sound of leaves closed in, immediately red lit eyes opened in the distance, watching every movement that the trembling, old man did. He ran hearing the deafening sound of paws closing in on him. Dumbledore saw his ancient doorway which led to warmth and safety, he was almost through the door when the creature leapt over his head, showing the muscular body powered by a craving for food, pouncing on Dumbledore in a flash. Gone…

ROBERT CLARKE (12)
The Appleton School, Benfleet

Three Pigs All For Me!

He saw them: the three pigs. They didn't know; they thought they were safe. Slowly and quietly he tiptoed round the newly built house, working out his plan. Dinner. It's all he could think about. 'Three pigs, all for me!' he whispered to himself. *Knock, knock.* Who was at the door? It was the wolf, all dressed up so the pigs wouldn't know it was him. The three pigs weren't stupid, they knew it was him. However, the wolf was too fast. He jumped at them showing all his teeth and within an instant… dead.

Olivia Gilbey (12)
The Appleton School, Benfleet

Helplessness

The megalomaniac devil unleashed the beast inside of him. Enraged, he released the soul-eating hounds upon the victims. Prepared to leave their life, they closed their eyes and whispered prayers as the creatures advanced rapidly. The end was closing in on them; for it was nigh. With blood-red anger in the devil's eyes and sinister, heart-stopping smirk, the prey turned to ashes in an instant. Gone. An evil cackle came from the devilish monster through the grit of his teeth. He leaned forwards and maliciously blew: the ashes drifted away. He spat, 'Puny mortals!'

Josh Budd (13)
The Appleton School, Benfleet

Sweet Guilt

The children approached the house dropping their last few breadcrumbs. They walked inside, the house was empty, the boy licked his lips and sat down at the table with a thump. The little girl looked around; she grew suspicious, wondering why somebody would have a home like that, it was made of marshmallows, popcorn and much more. Moments passed and the guilt of being in someone's home began to grow inside the girl's stomach. Then suddenly a noise. Somebody was there watching them waiting.

GRACE FULLER (12)
The Appleton School, Benfleet

Fate

He pushed open the door, slowly revealing what was waiting for him. The stench hit him like a slap round the face. The smell of rotting bodies was unbearable but he pushed on. His eyes watered uncontrollably causing him to stumble about blindly, tripping over bodies as he went. Something snapped behind him but when he turned around there was nothing there. Something was following him. He could feel its eerie presence. He sprinted down the corridor and up the dusty winding staircase. He knew that when he reached the top he would meet the same fate as the others.

JESSICA BROWN (12)
The Appleton School, Benfleet

DRIFTING APART

She woke up in her chair. She could smell them coming. Cold laughter filled the air as they approached the cottage. Thick fog surrounded the house greeting the children. Lured inside, the wolf howled. The sly prey hid. Not a problem, she could find them, she never lost one. The witch cackled, she dug her claws into the bodies and flung them into the oven. The children's screams filled the woods. The heat soaked them. Another dinner prepared. She opened the oven to find her worst nightmare; only one child in the oven. Not for long. She left the house.

TIFFANY MARSDEN-CARLETON (12)
The Appleton School, Benfleet

LONE WOLF

The wolf howled mournfully, hoping, praying his pack would reply. No answer. Admitting defeat, he turned, wandered aimlessly into the forest. He was lost, and being a young wolf, had never been alone before, and was rather nervous. The slightest sound, and he would flee the scene. A twig snapped. Instead of running, he froze. A horrid feeling crept down his spine. He could feel a presence. An evil presence. Panic gripped him like an invisible hand, immobilising him. His cry echoed through the desolate trees, haunting the place for evermore. His spirit lingered with the ones who took him.

ELLA SQUIRES (12)
The Appleton School, Benfleet

THE GHASTLY GUST

The wind flew through the abandoned house, pushing out all of the spirits lurking inside. All but one, this spirit's dark magic surrounding it, burning the touch of the ghastly gust. The door creaked open to reveal an empty room filled with smoke. But where had the smoke come from? Up the stairs maybe? A rusted, steel door opened just a crack, smoke gushing out of the miniscule opening. A transparent hand poked out, smashing the ancient door into the crumbling wall. A huge gust of ash-grey smoke flew, out of the space where the door once was.

KIERA MCDANIEL (12)
The Appleton School, Benfleet

THE CANDY HOUSE

The candy house gleamed in the sunlight as Hansel and Gretel crept round to the front, nibbling on the walls. But when they reached the front door, two withered hands tugged them into the house, throwing Hansel into a pan and Gretel into a cupboard. A sharp pain came to her shoulder as she hit the back of it, but as soon as she had the strength, she kicked the door; it was sent flying open. Gretel lashed out at an old witch and the witch fell back, being the thing Gretel wanted her to be: dead. As was Hansel.

EVIE FAIRBAIRN (12)
The Appleton School, Benfleet

THE WOODS

Nobody knew when the woods were planted or the rumours started. There were many tales of what happened if anyone entered the woods: curses, hauntings and plagues on the home of the trespasser. Nobody dared take the risk but many would question the tales. Little Tommy wanted an adventure. So he entered the woods; it was the biggest mistake of his life. His poor parents went insane looking for the child. Leading to the woods, fresh footprints explained everything.

A few nights later came a chilling scream from the boy's home. The first haunting, so the tales had been true.

HANNAH REYNOLDS (13)
The Appleton School, Benfleet

THE EVIL WITHIN

As Hansel and Gretel approached the house, they realised something: it was made of candy. They crept forward, intending to have some bites. A voice called to them, inviting them inside. The door slammed. There was nobody there so the children backed away, straight into the hard iron bars of the cage. The witch lit the stove and fire raged, but the door crashed open. Their father cut the screaming witch in two then closed in on the children a mad glint in his eye. They ran as fast as they could but the evil could not be stopped.

ALEX CLAYTON (12)
The Appleton School, Benfleet

115

THE BLOOD DOLL

A doll that looked so innocent sat in the corner with a sinister smile. In his hand laid a knife; the blade painted with blood. In front of him was a pale corpse. Slowly, the doll stood up. His plastic heart beating inside of his silicone body and his menacing mind plotting another horrific murder. Then, within seconds, the lights switched off, and the doll was nowhere in sight. I felt an instant pain and faintly saw the blood bleeding from my heart. Then before I took my last breath, the words 'blood doll' howled through my ears.

MITCHELL THOMAS OLA BALOGUN (12)
The Appleton School, Benfleet

OUT OF THE WOODS INTO THE OVEN

A deceiving smile stood in the doorway: red lips, grey hair and a chuckle to hide from. The siblings never to have left the forest, pulled with bear-like claws into the sweet house. She (the hag) filled them up; refusing their offer to leave. Hansel felt her lukewarm breath on his arm. She wanted to eat him. The brother and sister were tricked into the oven. They were vulnerable but, the pair brushed open the door with a devilish look. The hag was going to be their dinner. Left to burn but she was heard screaming from miles. Lifeless.

CHARLOTTE MCDONAGH (13)
The Appleton School, Benfleet

THE END OF THE WITCH

The house was made of candy but what was inside was far from sweet: the witch. Hansel and Gretel stood in front of the candy cottage waiting for the moment they could vanquish the beast inside. The witch had kidnapped most of the town's children; enough was enough. They crept inside and shut the door. Inside, the witch was asleep, lying next to the cage where she kept the children. Hansel grabbed the knife. There was a scream. She's gone. Dead.

ELLIE FRENCH (13)
The Appleton School, Benfleet

THE CANNIBAL

The giant could smell the young boy and was ready to eat him. Breathing heavily, the young boy was ready to run and gain his freedom away from this cannibal beast. The giant shouted and screamed for his prey: he knew the young boy was close. Would he survive? He continued searching and shouting, hoping the young boy would give in. Suddenly, a noise. *Clash!* The young boy had dropped a plate. The giant ran towards the noise and found the young boy. He screamed and screamed for help, but nobody came. *Gulp.* He was eaten.

JACIE HARRIS (13)
The Appleton School, Benfleet

BRICKS AND BONES

Death hung in the air. He had already targeted his first three victims: some young pigs hidden in a brick house. Breathing heavily, the wolf approached the house, preparing his lungs for the task ahead. Lighting the fire using sticks and hay from their previous houses, they thought they were safe. But, little did they know, they were not. The wolf filled up his lungs and began to blow the house; with three puffs the pigs were crushed under the brick. The wolf opened its mouth and swallowed the victims whole. Nothing escaped the vicious wolf's death-inducing jaws. Nothing. Nothing!

REMI ROSARIO (13)
The Appleton School, Benfleet

THE DEMON AND THE DOOR

Dizzy and terrified, Shannon laid beyond a rotted door. This was her greatest fear but Shannon faced it and she turned the way of the door. Turned the handle. It screamed like terrified mice. Meanwhile, the demon got closer. Shannon had killed many insects: spiders, ants and a cockroach but nothing as big as the creature she was staring at. Shannon was in the room. She looked up and saw dangling bodies! Blood dripping, she screamed and a deep voice asked her, 'You want to join them?' Shannon closed her eyes and that was the last time she did.

JOSHUA SMITH (13)
The Appleton School, Benfleet

TRUST MAKES BETRAYAL

She approached the sweet smelling house, wearing her bloodstained hoodie. The wicked laughter inside the home told her what was happening; the children were going to die. The blonde haired girl rushed to the door. She yanked the door knob and rushed inside to find two children: Hansel and Gretel. But not just that, the malicious, ancient witch was in the oven! The children were supposed to be in there! The girl, with the beautiful blonde locks, turned around and ran for her life. She could hear loud footsteps behind her. Getting louder and louder. Then silence.

DAISY PRICE (13)
The Appleton School, Benfleet

STRANDED DEEP ALONE

Stranded: alone on the island. Hunting for food and resources. I was stalking the unknown. Bow and arrows equipped in hand, waiting for the right moment to strike. It was hard to see my prey at night. There! I saw an unknown creature edging its way out of the cave. Aim! Fire! I missed. Now I wasn't the hunter; I was the hunted. I dropped my bow and ran for my life. The creature was charging at me. Dodging the oncoming trees, I could hear the beast was gaining ground. I was still alive; not for long. I fell, lifeless.

JAMIE EVERETT (13)
The Appleton School, Benfleet

Untitled

The giant raised his nose – he could smell something. Fear. He towered over Jack, dwarfing him. Jack raced for a large mouse-hole, twisting and turning through colossal table legs. The hole must have been only a few hundred metres away. The thumping footsteps of the gigantic giant stopped; everything was silent. Jack's heart was pumping. He was nervous. Petrified. Unable to move. Paralysed. Horrified at the situation, Jack dashed for the hole, as fast as a cheetah he leapt over the massive stone slab, into the giant mouse hole! He was safe. For now.

JOSEPH FLYNN (13)
The Appleton School, Benfleet

Asylum

Blood seeped out of my eyes. My body submerged in blood. My bones shattered to shreds; my mind dragged to Hell, I used the last slithers of my hope to drag myself sorrowfully with my broken arms. The screams of the mad men stalked my presence. A sight, a thought emerged into the peripheral of my mind … Lights flickering. A monster creeping, later killing me. I felt I had a chance, slim but still there. I reached the door and twisted it vigorously. It wouldn't budge, I peered back to find the face of a mad man smiling creepily…

NATHAN BOACHIE
The Coopers Company & Coborn School, Upminster

NEIGHBOURS?

In all the time that I lived alone, I swear to God I've closed more doors than I have opened. With a shadow walking around the streets suspiciously disappearing, the streets became a chess game: one wrong move and game over. Mama always told me these stories about the shadows coming alive. And at night you never knew what was coming. In the middle of the night I turned and battled my way through the dark to see in the mirror, a man – one blink and I then saw… blood. Was it now my turn to vanish?

EMMANUEL LAWAL
The Coopers Company & Coborn School, Upminster

LIVING METAL

The dark metal creature rose out of its tomb. Lots of Imperial soldiers firing their guns, but of course the puny weapons didn't even make a scratch on the evil monster's face. It squeezed its hands around one of the soldier's necks until blood and meat oozed out. Then the monstrous machine swung round with its pulsing weapon. The light was illuminating his terrifying death mask as the tester weapon turned all his shocked foes to ash. He will rule the lost tomb world of Medusa. No more Ogotath the Overlord. Now it is Hysrek, the creature's turn…

JOSEPH EVANS (12)
The King John School, Benfleet

THE BEAST!

I had done it. I had finally slain the beast that had killed many people on Earth. In fact it had killed everyone but me. Why did I do it? Now I'm on my own. Spending the rest of my days all alone. The beast, funnily enough, was a gigantic hamster with magical powers and I was the only person brave enough to go up to it as it slept. My spear went straight through its heart killing it instantly. Shame that I have no one to tell the story of my bravery to, oh well.

LILY CAPON (11)
The King John School, Benfleet

THE GREMLINS AND THE SCIENTISTS

Dr Daniels was a scientist, and very good too. However, every night, when he would leave research alone, things went missing. Doctor Daniels had enough of this! He set up a trap in his lab and waited until dusk.
A few moments after dusk, the gremlins came. Two foot tall creatures with blistery, red skin and charcoal eyes. These were the creatures taking his research but for what? He got up to leave but his glasses dropped! Doctor Daniels froze. The gremlins started their ascend towards him. There were more than he thought all rushing towards him. What would happen?

SERA MENEZES (13)
The Palmer Catholic Academy, Ilford

CHASE OF THE WOLVES

The three wolves whimpered, as they sniffed a pig two miles away. It's surely the notorious pig that escaped. Trying to avoid the chance of being eaten, they went into the hidden cellar of the house. Silence. A temporary luxury. Tails tight between their little legs, they waited. Suddenly, a blood-curdling roar was heard. It's arrived. The cellar door lifted, letting a shaft of light penetrate the darkness. They ran. A cry, a roar. Their youngest brother's gone. Behind the safety of some miles of trees, they're met with the unwelcome sight of the ravenous pig devouring their brother.

KAJAANI RAVEENDRAN (13)
The Palmer Catholic Academy, Ilford

THE WITCH HUNTERS!

There was once a forest full of monsters and magic that lay on the boundaries of a city. One day two children, brother and sister, were left in the woods; an evil short-sighted witch sensed their fear, distress and hunger. So she quickly constructed a house made of gingerbread. Shortly, the young siblings arrived to her abode. 'Why hello there little ones, are you hungry?' said the witch.
To her surprise a gruff voice replied, 'Keine,' and a mighty whoosh sent her head tumbling. The blind witch couldn't see over the disguise. The witch hunters: Hansel and Gretel left.

SINAN KHAN (12)
The Palmer Catholic Academy, Ilford

THE PREDATOR WHO BECAME PREY

The fearful girl heard suspicious rustling from the bushes. She scanned the area, but failed to spot anything, until suddenly, she saw a flash of silver amongst the bushes. The girl knew she was prey, waiting to be violently intercepted by the lone wolf that crept around the obscure bushes. Panicking, the girl tried to think of an escape plan, however, as she tried to stay composed, panic took over and soon erupted out of her like a volcano. She rapidly started to flee, her predator close behind. Abruptly, an axe flew towards the wolf, and the hunt was over…

AJEET SINGH (12)
The Palmer Catholic Academy, Ilford

THE ESCAPE

I turned around. Gretel was there catching up. She clasped my hand. I felt wrinkles sanding away my skin. I felt long, thin nails digging into my veins.
A lucky escape from the depraved witch. The confectionery on the house was tempting. Lucky me. I didn't eat them.
Suddenly I felt a cold shiver through the back of my spine, as I looked up I saw a razor-sharp nose and a pair of bulging eyes that stared right through me. Gretel started cackling loudly. As I looked at her, frightened, I could see a crumb on her mouth.

SOFIA LODHI (13)
The Palmer Catholic Academy, Ilford

THE DEFENDER OF THE BRIDGE – A TWIST ON THE THREE BILLY GOATS GRUFF

Tap, bang, bang and there he was. We stood face to face and he stared at me with burning eyes. He stood his ground and bowed his head, slowly shaking it. He laughed menacingly. Suddenly, he charged. The tips of his pointed horns facing towards me! The horns approached fast, hitting me in the stomach. I stumbled backwards, tripping and falling over the bridge. I caught a glimpse of those evil goats eating my grass, then I was engulfed by the deep, blue abyss. I sank further and further until complete darkness. I closed my eyes waiting for the inevitable.

AMY POOLE (13)
The Palmer Catholic Academy, Ilford

THE CURSED FOREST

You never know. The dangers of the forest, no one ever escaped, that is true. However, no one knows why. Maybe it's the ferocious creatures lurking in the darkness of the mournful trees who follow you with their soulless eyes. The smoky darkness that consumes your soul and the grasping arms of the earth beneath. The last person to go there was just a small child unaware of the danger. Walking around knowing nothing. He wouldn't escape. No one escaped. The forest makes sure of it. He lived there for years, losing his sanity. The one child was me.

PATRICK OLUWADAMILOLA MATULUKO (12)
The Palmer Catholic Academy, Ilford

Hansel And Gretel

There lived a boy and a girl called Hansel and Gretel. Their stepmother was a witch and she acted nice to them, but in fact she really hated them. She sent them to the forest where she summoned a nasty, greedy, sly fox because she wanted them dead! But the fox disobeyed her. She got very angry so she turned into the fox herself and then she went to the forest which had a foresty smell to it. She snapped them right into her lair and she was extremely happy that she had killed them. How cruel is that?

Colin Haye (12)
Trinity School, Brentwood

Not So Sweet

Once there lived two girls. Everyone loved these two girls. Their family loved them to bits.
One day these two lovely girls went for a walk. They had not been told to beware of the gate. Legend has it that anyone who went through the gate turned bad. These girls had no idea and went through the gate. They were not so lovely after their walk. They left a trail of destruction. Their poor mother and father, nobody knows where they are. These girls still live, causing suffering wherever they go, those sweet girls are not so sweet anymore.

Ivy Samuel (12)
Trinity School, Brentwood

JUSTIN: RISING FROM THE DEAD

The air was cold as Abbey walked through the pitch-black, stormy graveyard. Suddenly, she heard a rustling sound and it got louder and louder as she walked closer to it. She pushed the trees and the sticky branches, which were covered in blood, and saw Justin Bieber, a bloody knife lodged in-between his ribs.

(Abbey's point of view) I walked closer and sat next to him and I suddenly felt the thick air hit my face.

Next thing I knew I felt a cold, stiff hand on my lap. OMG he wasn't dead. Justin pleaded, 'Help me please.'

ABIRAMI SATHYAMURTHI (12)
Valentines High School, Ilford

YOUNG WRITERS
INFORMATION

We hope you have enjoyed reading this book – and
that you will continue to in the coming years.

If you're a young writer who enjoys reading and creative writing, or
the parent of an enthusiastic poet or story writer, do visit our website
www.youngwriters.co.uk. Here you will find free
competitions, workshops and games, as well as
recommended reads, a poetry glossary and our blog.

If you would like to order further copies of this book, or any of
our other titles give us a call or visit **www.youngwriters.co.uk**.

Young Writers
Remus House
Coltsfoot Drive
Peterborough
PE2 9BF

(01733) 890066 / 898110
info@youngwriters.co.uk